WILDFIRE HEARTS SERIES #3

SMOKE AND Surrender

VA BROWNING

Contents

1st edition – 2026

The Lightning-Struck Pine

♥

Emma

The dirt road twisted through ponderosa pines like it was trying to lose me. I cranked the steering wheel left, then right, my SUV's tires spitting gravel as I climbed higher into the Colorado mountains. Each switchback took me farther from civilization, farther from Seattle, farther from the mess of my life. The GPS had given up ten minutes ago, leaving me with Dorothy Clairmore's handwritten directions clutched in one hand.

Third cattle guard, sharp right at the lightning-struck pine, follow the creek.

The paper felt solid in my hand, a relic from a world before satellites dictated our every turn. My entire career had been built on predictability—on metrics and market research, on algorithms that could forecast consumer behavior down to the decimal point. It was a safe, sterile world of spreadsheets and certain outcomes, a fortress I'd constructed to keep out the emotional chaos of a childhood spent waiting for a father who was never really there. This road, with its lack of cell service and its trust in a lightning-struck pine, was the antithesis of that life. It was terrifying. And it was freeing.

Windows down. Mountain air rushed in—thin and sharp, carrying pine sap and something wild I couldn't name. My lungs ached from the altitude, or maybe from holding my breath since I'd crossed the Colorado state line.

There. The lightning-struck pine stood as a charcoal-blackened sentinel, one splintered arm pointing the way down a track I'd have otherwise missed. I turned, and the road narrowed to barely more than two tire tracks through tall grass.

Then I saw it.

The A-frame cabin rose from a clearing like it had grown there. Cedar logs the color of honey, a green metal roof that matched the surrounding pines, and a wall of windows facing west toward mountains that scraped the sky. My foot came off the gas. The SUV rolled to a stop in the gravel drive.

I sat there, engine ticking, staring at what would be home for the next three months. No. Not home. Just a rental. A place to write. A place to think. A place to forget about—

Stop.

I grabbed my purse and climbed out. The silence hit me like a physical thing. No traffic. No sirens. No neighbor's TV bleeding through thin apartment walls. Just wind moving through pine branches and somewhere beyond the trees, water running over rocks.

The key waited under a fake rock by the front door—the kind of trust that only existed in places like this. The lock turned smooth, and the door swung open. The air left my lungs in a quiet whoosh. It was all one room, a cavern of honey-colored wood and light that made my chest ache. It was a specific kind of ache, one I recognized from novels but had never felt myself. Hope. And it was terrifying. Hope was my mother's poison. It was the thing that kept her waiting by a window for a man who had already chosen the horizon. Hope was a quiet, slow-burning fire that left nothing but ash.

To the right, a kitchen with butcher block counters invited use, its gas stove a relic from an era before planned obsolescence. Straight ahead, a stone fireplace soared to the peaked ceiling, a silent stone hearth waiting for a flame. That wall of windows I'd seen from outside flooded everything with afternoon light that turned the wood floors to gold.

My purse landed on the counter with a soft thud. I drifted toward the light, drawn to the wall of windows like a moth. I stopped, my hand hovering just above the glass. The view wasn't a picture; it was a presence. Mountains crowded the horizon, their snow-capped peaks looking brittle and sharp against a sky bruised with the promise of rain. An eagle scribbled a lazy circle overhead.

Perfect. It was perfect.

Which meant I'd find a way to ruin it. That's what I did with perfect things.

I turned from the view and climbed the ladder to the loft bedroom. Just a full bed with a quilt that looked handmade, a simple dresser, and a window that would wake me with sunrise whether I wanted it or not. I'd slept in worse places, and better.

None of them had ever felt like—

Stop.

Back downstairs, I hauled my suitcases from the SUV. Three months of clothes, though I'd probably wear the same jeans and cardigan every day. Who was going to see me out here? I hung things in the small closet, folded underwear into dresser drawers, and set my toiletries on the bathroom's single shelf.

The laptop bag came last. I carried it to the desk by the windows—clearly where Dorothy intended guests to write or work. The desk was nothing special, just pine boards and metal legs, but positioned to capture that view. I pulled out my MacBook, its aluminum surface covered in coffee shop stickers from Seattle. Pike Place Market. Victrola. Storyville. All the places I'd tried to write and failed.

The laptop hummed to life. I opened a new document, watched the cursor blink against white emptiness.

My fingers hovered over the keys. Three months. I'd told myself three months was enough time to write a book. To prove I was more than spreadsheets and marketing campaigns. To justify walking away from—

"But you're up for Senior Director."

Martin Jensen's voice echoed in my memory. My boss—former boss—sitting behind his glass desk in the corner office overlooking Elliott Bay. His confusion when I'd placed my resignation letter in front of him.

"I need to take some time. Focus on a personal project."

"We can give you a leave of absence. Three months, full benefits."

"That's generous, but—"

"Emma, you're our best strategic mind. The Nordstrom campaign alone—"

"I know."

I'd known. Senior Director of Strategic Marketing at thirty. Six figures. Corner office waiting. Everything my mother had pushed me toward since I'd declared my creative writing minor "impractical."

I had felt nothing. Absolutely nothing. And I had a couple of years worth of savings to get me through this test as an author.

The cursor blinked. Blinked. Blinked.

I slammed the laptop shut and pushed back from the desk. Coffee. I needed coffee. The kitchen revealed a drip machine that belonged in a museum, but it worked. While it gurgled and hissed, I found Dorothy's welcome note magneted to the fridge.

Dear Emma, Welcome to Ponderosa Cabin! The wifi password is "creekside2019" and yes, it's slow, but it works. Don't forget to check the propane tank gauge weekly. I've left you a map of local hiking trails—the Copper Peak trail is lovely this time of year. The general store in town delivers on Wednesdays if you call ahead. If you need anything, my nephew James Drake has the ranch about four miles east. Good people. Enjoy your summer of writing! -Dorothy

I turned to the wall where a topographic map hung in a rustic frame. Red dotted lines marked hiking trails with names like Devil's Ridge, Widow's Walk, and Copper Peak. My finger traced the lines, measuring distances. I'd brought my boots. I'd hike every morning, clear my head, come back and write.

That was the plan. Plans were good. Plans kept you from thinking about—

Gray eyes. Laughter that rumbled like distant thunder. Hands that—

"Stop."

I spoke aloud to the empty cabin. My voice sounded thin in all that space. I poured coffee into a mug decorated with painted pinecones and carried it to the window seat. The cushions sank under my weight, cradling me in a way that suggested hundreds of other guests had sat here, watching the same mountains, wrestling with their own demons.

The coffee was terrible. I'd forgotten to pack good beans, and Dorothy had left Folgers. It tasted like burned dirt, but it was hot and familiar. I pulled my knees to my chest and looked out at the wall of pines surrounding the cabin.

I didn't need to close my eyes to see him. Portland, five years ago. A hotel bar that smelled of stale beer and rain. Three days that had burned down the perfectly constructed framework of my life.

I could still see him across that hotel bar. The Oregon Wildfire Management Conference—I'd been there presenting Jensen & Associates' crisis communication strategies. He'd been there because he fought fires from the sky, jumping from planes into infernos with nothing but a parachute and a prayer.

"That seat taken?"

"It's a free country."

"Wyatt Drake. You look like you'd rather be anywhere but here."

"Emma Reed. And you're right."

The memory was sharp enough to cut. How easy it had been. How right. We'd talked until the bar closed. Argued about books—he'd actually read *Pride and Prejudice*, claiming Elizabeth should have seen Darcy's worth from the start. I'd laughed harder than I had in months. But it wasn't just the laughter. It was the shock of being truly seen. With Brandon, with my colleagues, even with my friends, I was a collection of roles: the fiancée, the strategic mind, the reliable one. But Wyatt... he hadn't seen any of those things. He'd looked past the carefully constructed facade and seen *me*. The girl who scribbled story ideas on napkins and believed in Darcy's redemption. It was a terrifying intimacy I hadn't experienced before or since, a ghost of connection I'd been running from for five years.

My phone had buzzed with texts from Brandon. My fiancé. Sweet, stable, boring Brandon with his law degree and his boat shoes and his mother who'd already booked the country club for our June wedding. Brandon, who felt less like a partner and more like another metric I'd achieved. Another box checked on my mother's list of what constituted a "practical life." The engagement itself had been a strategic marketing campaign—his proposal at the Space Needle, perfectly timed for sunset, the ring what my mother would have chosen. I'd said yes because it made sense on paper, because I'd been sleepwalking through my own life for so long I'd forgotten what it felt like to be awake.

I'd turned the phone face-down and ordered another whiskey.

Three perfect, terrible, life-ruining days. Days when I'd finally woken up. And then I'd left without saying goodbye.

I'd gone back to Seattle. Back to Brandon and his boat shoes. Back to the fortress I'd built. I'd tried to slip back into sleep, to pretend Portland had been a fever dream. But I'd been sleepwalking ever since—through the rest of the engagement, through Brandon's mother's increasingly detailed wedding plans, through my mother's satisfied nods as she watched me choose the practical path she'd always prescribed. Even breaking off the engagement six months later had felt like something happening to someone else. I'd stood in Brandon's tasteful living room, the ring in my palm, and watched him look more relieved than heartbroken.

"You were never really here," he'd said. He wasn't wrong.

I set the coffee on the windowsill and walked outside. The deck wrapped around two sides of the cabin, the boards weathered silver. I followed it to where I could hear water. A path through the trees led to the creek—really more of a stream, running fast with snowmelt. Flat rocks created natural seats along the bank.

I sat on one, the stone cold through my jeans. The water was so clear I could count the pebbles on the bottom. Hypnotic. Peaceful.

This could be enough. Three months of this—the silence, the mountains, the blank page waiting to be filled. I didn't need more. I didn't need permanence. I didn't need—

A stick snapped in the woods behind me. My head whipped around, but it was just a deer. A doe, picking her way through the underbrush, ears swiveling like satellite dishes. Our eyes met. The deer evaluated me, decided I wasn't a threat, and continued toward the creek.

I held my breath as the doe drank, water dripping from her black nose. Then, as suddenly as she'd appeared, she bounded back into the trees, white tail flashing.

The woods went quiet again.

I stood, brushed off my jeans, and walked back to the cabin. I had to finish unpacking. Groceries to put away—I'd stopped in Copper Ridge, endured the stares of locals wondering who the stranger was. A week's worth of pasta, canned soup, wine. I wasn't here to cook elaborate meals.

I was here to write. To finally finish something. To prove I could.

Back at the desk, I opened the laptop again. The cursor still blinked at me, patient and demanding.

My fingers found the keys.

Three months. I can do this until Lily's wedding and then see if it's working.

I stared at the sentence. It wasn't the opening to a novel. It was a promise. Or maybe a lie.

I highlighted the words and hit delete.

The blank page stared back.

I closed the laptop again, gentler this time. Tomorrow. I'd start tomorrow. Tonight, I'd settle in. Make dinner. Maybe build a fire even though it wasn't really cold enough. Drink wine on the deck and watch the stars come out—there would be stars here, wouldn't there? Not like Seattle's orange-tinted sky.

I stood at the window, watching shadows lengthen across the valley. The mountains were turning purple in the evening light, their peaks catching the last of the sun. Beautiful. Heartbreaking. Temporary.

"This could be home."

The words escaped before I could stop them. They hung in the air like an accusation. Home was a concept for other people. People who stayed. People who committed. People who didn't have engagement rings hidden in their purses while they fell in love with gray-eyed smoke jumpers in Portland hotel bars.

I pressed my palm flat against the window glass. Cool. Solid. Real.

"This could be enough," I said, speaking to my reflection, to the mountains, to the gathering dusk. "For three months."

Silver Frames and Stale Beer

♥

Emma

A box gave way, the tape surrendering with a tired rip. Paperbacks—a dozen of them—fanned across the floor. Cracked spines, faded covers, the kind of grocery-store romances I'd built a career marketing and a personal life avoiding. The kind I'd sworn I'd never write.

My laptop sat on the desk like a loaded gun.

Two years. Two years of opening that file, staring at the cursor, closing it again. My agent Jane had stopped asking for updates six months ago. Now she just sent encouraging emojis and links to articles about "overcoming creative blocks."

I stacked the paperbacks on the coffee table and turned to the mantel. Dorothy's photos watched me unpack, a timeline of devotion carved in silver frames. Young Dorothy in a white sundress, laughing as a man—her husband, had to be—dipped her backward on this very deck. The same couple, middle-aged now, raising a toast beside the fireplace. Elderly hands clasped on a porch swing I'd noticed outside, still there but weathered gray.

My fingers traced the final frame. Dorothy alone, silver-haired, feeding birds from the deck railing. The date on the back: three years ago.

Nothing lasts.

The smile on Dorothy's face was serene, but all I saw was my mother's smile after my father left for good—a brave, brittle thing pasted over a cavern of loneliness. A cold dread washed over me. This wasn't just a story of a long love; it was a preview of the inevitable ending I feared most. The woman left behind.

I pulled my hand back. These weren't my memories to touch.

The laptop screen bloomed to life at my touch. Jane's latest email sat at the top of my inbox, subject line: *URGENT: Publisher Interest - Need Update*

Em, Hartwell Press loved your sample chapters. They want the full manuscript by December. This is THE opportunity. Please tell me you're close? -J

December. Five months to write an ending I couldn't envision.

I opened the manuscript file. Chapter 15 stared back—my wildland firefighter hero walking away from my marketing specialist heroine for the third time. I'd written him leaving six different ways. Deleted them all. Started over. He kept leaving.

Art imitating life.

My hands curled into fists. I wouldn't think about it. About him. About three weeks ago when everything—

The memory crashed through.

***

The dress had been a mistake. Soft blue, the kind that brought out the green in my eyes. I'd stood in front of the hotel mirror that evening, smoothing the fabric over my hips, telling myself I wasn't dressing for anyone. Just showing up for Lily. My friend. Who deserved support at her engagement party and I was in town partly for her wedding as well as my adventure into being an author.

The Copper Ridge Community Center had glowed with string lights, laughter spilling out the doors into the warm evening. I'd sat in my rental car for ten minutes, watching couples stream inside, before forcing myself to move.

"Emma!" Lily had appeared the moment I'd walked in, radiant in red, pulling me into a hug that smelled like champagne and happiness. "You came!"

"Of course I came."

Mason had joined us, his arm around Lily's waist, that quiet intensity softened by obvious love. "Good to see you, Emma. My brothers are around somewhere—"

"I should find the bar." The words had tumbled out too fast. "Get you two something?"

Lily's eyes had narrowed slightly, reading the panic I couldn't quite hide. "Emma—"

"Champagne? Wine? Back in a minute."

I'd fled before she could answer, weaving through the crowd toward the makeshift bar. All of Copper Ridge had been there—Ruby from the salon, the Pattersons, Dr. Sarah, people whose names I'd since learned but whose faces blurred together in my need to find an escape route.

The punch bowl had stood unguarded. I'd ladled the pink liquid into a plastic cup, my hand steady despite the tremor in my chest. The stuff had tasted like pure sugar and regret.

"Well, well, well. Hello there stranger."

The voice had hit me between the shoulder blades. I'd turned, and there he was. A man I never thought I would see again. How is he here, now, when I need to be working not daydreaming about...

Wyatt Drake. Five years older but looking exactly the same. Sun-bleached hair a little too long, that stubborn wave falling across his forehead. Gray eyes that had haunted my dreams and ruined me for every man since. Worn jeans and a button-down shirt that stretched across shoulders I could still feel under my palms if I closed my eyes.

"Wyatt." His name had scraped my throat raw.

"Emma." He'd stepped closer, too close, close enough that I could smell him—pine and smoke and something indefinably him . "I couldn't believe it when Mason said Lily's friend Emma Reed was coming. I could only hope it was actually the Emma that I remembered."

"Just for the summer."

"Right. Working on a book." The words had carried an edge sharp enough to cut.

The crowd had pressed around us, oblivious to the grenade he'd just pulled the pin on.

"I don't—"

"Three days, Emma. What happened? You just vanished."

My cup had trembled. Pink punch had sloshed dangerously close to the rim. "You knew what you were getting into. A weekend—"

"Don't." His voice had dropped low, dangerous. "Don't you dare pretend that it was just a weekend."

"What do you want me to say?" The words had come out louder than intended. A few heads had turned. "That I'm sorry? That I should have—"

"Explained? Said goodbye? Given me a reason?"

"You were leaving anyway!" The accusation had burst out of me. "Alaska, remember? Another season, another state, another—"

He'd stepped closer still, his chest nearly touching mine. "That's what you told yourself, right? That I'd leave eventually, so why bother?"

The party noise dissolved into a high-pitched hum, the sound of my own blood rushing in my ears. The world narrowed to his face, the anger there, the hurt.

Panic clawed at my throat. My carefully constructed identity—Emma Reed, successful marketing director from Seattle, the capable friend, the writer—was dissolving under the weight of a hundred pairs of eyes. In this room, I wasn't any of those things. I was just a woman in a messy, public drama with a man who looked at me like I'd set his world on fire and then walked away. I felt stripped bare, judged, and my only instinct was to build the walls higher, find an escape route, and disappear all over again.

"You're here. In my town. At my brother's engagement party."

"Lily's my friend."

"And I'm Mason's brother. So what do we do, Emma? Pretend we're strangers? Pretend Portland never happened?"

"Yes." The word had come out strangled. "That's exactly what we do."

Something had shifted in his expression. The anger had dissolved into something worse—hurt. Raw and undisguised.

"You're good at pretending, aren't you?" His voice had gone quiet, which was somehow worse than the anger. "Pretending you don't feel things. Pretending you don't want things. Pretending you're fine alone."

"Stop."

"Tell me you've been happy." He'd searched my face. "These five years. Tell me you found what you were looking for."

I couldn't. The truth was a stone in my throat, too heavy to lift, too sharp to swallow.

"That's what I thought." He'd stepped back, and the loss of his proximity had felt like drowning. "Enjoy the party, Emma. I'm sure you'll be gone soon enough."

He'd walked away, leaving me standing there with a cup of too-sweet punch and the entire population of Copper Ridge staring.

***

I slammed the laptop shut hard enough to rattle Dorothy's photos. My hands shook. Three weeks, and the memory still had the power to make my stomach clench. I could still feel the weight of every eye in that room, the sudden silence when our voices rose. Lily's pity in the bathroom doorway. The way Ruby from the salon wouldn't meet my gaze at the general store the next morning. Everyone knew.

I stood, paced to the window, pressed my forehead against the cool glass. The mountains stared back, impassive and eternal. They'd been here before Dorothy and her husband. Before their love story played out in these rooms. They'd be here after I left.

Nothing lasts.

Except Dorothy and her husband had lasted. Forty-three years, according to the date on their wedding photo. Forty-three years of summers and winters in this cabin. Of morning coffee on the deck and evening fires. Of choosing each other over and over until death finally parted them.

My phone buzzed. A text from Lily.

How's the writing going? Miss you already.

I typed back: *Good. Quiet here. Perfect for focus.*

Three lies in seven words. A personal record.

My hands needed work, something to do besides tremble. I tore into the next box. Kitchen supplies. Mismatched mugs and scratched pans tumbled onto the counter, each one worn with a history that wasn't mine.

The cast iron skillet weighed a ton. Someone—Dorothy probably—had seasoned it to a mirror shine. How many meals had it made? How many mornings of eggs and bacon while her husband read the paper? How many anniversaries, birthdays, ordinary Tuesdays that added up to a life?

Stop it.

I shoved the skillet into a cabinet. Next box. Linens. The scent of lavender bloomed from storage-soft towels. But it was the quilt, wrapped in crackling tissue paper, that stopped me. Handmade. Intricate. A wedding ring pattern stitched with a patience I couldn't imagine.

A note pinned to the tissue caught my eye. *My mother's wedding quilt. Please enjoy. -Dorothy*

The fabric felt like silk under my fingers. Someone had stitched this with love, every piece chosen with care. Interlocking circles that went on forever, no beginning, no end.

I spread it across the bed in the loft, smoothing out wrinkles that didn't exist. It transformed the simple space, made it feel like—

No. Not home. Just a nice rental. A place to write. Nothing more.

Back downstairs, I opened the laptop again. The cursor blinked at me, patient and accusing.

My firefighter hero stood at the edge of the page, ready to leave again. I'd written him a hundred different ways—bitter, resigned, hopeful, angry. He always left. She always let him.

Because that's what people did. They left. Even when they promised to stay, even when they said forever, they left. By choice or by chance or by the simple erosion of feelings that couldn't sustain themselves against reality.

My hands fell away from the keyboard. I couldn't write them a happy ending because I didn't believe in them. My hero kept leaving because, in my world, men always did. My father. And now Wyatt. The manuscript wasn't fiction; it was a prophecy I was writing in real-time. Every ending I wrote felt like a prophecy. Like admitting that some stories don't get happy endings, no matter how much you want them.

I scrolled back through the manuscript, past the failed endings, past the arguments and near-misses, until I found Chapter 8. The scene where Helena, my heroine, sat at a restaurant table across from her perfectly acceptable boyfriend, smiling through another dinner with his colleagues. Playing the role. Being the right kind of woman—supportive, pleasant, undemanding.

My chest tightened as I read my own words.

Helena laughed at the senior partner's joke, the sound hollow in her own ears. Across the table, David beamed at her, proud. She was performing well. That's what their relationship had become—a performance. He loved the version of her that showed up to these dinners, that nodded along to his career plans, that never asked for more than he was willing to give. The real Helena, the one who wanted wild conversations at 2 AM and spontaneous road trips and a man who looked at her like she was necessary to his breathing—that Helena had learned to stay quiet. She'd been underwater so long she'd forgotten what the surface looked like.

I sat back, the words blurring. That's what I'd done with Brandon. Two years of being the woman he needed—organized, professional, content with his careful plans and measured affection. Two years of drowning in shallow water, so slowly I hadn't noticed until I couldn't breathe.

And then Portland. Then Wyatt.

Three days that had felt like breaking the surface after being under too long. Three days of gasping in air I didn't know I'd been missing. Three days of being seen—really seen—by someone who didn't need me to be smaller or quieter or more convenient.

Cheating. That's what everyone called it. What I called it, in the dark hours when shame crawled up my throat.

But maybe it was something else. Maybe it was a drowning woman breaking a window to escape.

I looked at Helena on the page, still sitting at that dinner table, still pretending. In my first draft, I'd had her stay. Had her accept David's eventual proposal. Had her build a life on the foundation of hollowness because that's what good women did. They made it work. They didn't blow everything up chasing something as unreliable as air.

My fingers hovered over the keys. Then I started typing.

Helena set down her wine glass with a clarity that felt like surfacing. "Excuse me," she said, standing. David looked up, confused. "I need to—I'm sorry. I can't do this." She walked out of the restaurant into the cool night air, and for the first time in two years, she could breathe.

I stared at the words. It wasn't cheating that had ended my engagement. It was the moment before—the two years of slow suffocation, of being someone I wasn't, of accepting hollow when I was starving for whole.

The kiss was just the explosion. The catalyst. The desperate act of a woman who'd been underwater too long and finally, finally broke.

***

The afternoon sun had shifted, painting golden stripes across the floor. Dorothy's younger self smiled from the mantle, frozen in a moment of perfect happiness.

Had she known, that young bride, what she was signing up for? The fights that would come, the disappointments, the ordinary Wednesdays when love felt more like work than magic? Or had she just been young and foolish and brave enough to try?

I walked outside, needing air that didn't smell like memory. The deck boards creaked under my feet—a comfortable sound, like the cabin welcoming me. The porch swing hung in the corner, the same one from Dorothy's photos. I sat, setting it in gentle motion.

The mountains hadn't moved. The creek still sang its water song. An eagle circled overhead, riding thermals I couldn't see.

Three months. I had three months to write an ending, to figure out how to let my characters be happy. Three months to sit on this porch and pretend I belonged here. Three months to avoid Wyatt Drake and the questions in his gray eyes. I couldn't explain to him why I'd left him after the magic we shared.

The swing chains groaned softly. Back and forth, back and forth, marking time I couldn't get back and couldn't move forward.

My phone buzzed again. Another text from Lily.

Wedding planning is chaos. Thank god I have you for MOH duties. Dress shopping next weekend?

Maid of honor. Of course. Because the universe had a sense of humor, and that humor involved forcing me to stand beside Lily while Wyatt stood beside Mason. Matching positions, matching roles, pretending we were nothing to each other while everyone watched and remembered that night at the engagement party when our past had exploded like fireworks.

Can't wait, I typed back. Another lie. I was getting good at them.

The sun started its descent behind the peaks, painting everything gold and rose. Beautiful. Temporary. Like everything else.

I stood, walked inside, and stared at my laptop. At the life someone else had lived in these rooms. I could pretend for a while.

Pretend I didn't care about a man who jumped out of planes into wildfires. Even pretend I could write a happy ending. Even pretend this cabin was just a rental and not the first place that had ever felt like home.

The Twelve Days of Silence

♥

Emma

The coffee ran out first. Then the eggs. By Thursday morning, I'd eaten the last slice of bread and scraped peanut butter from an empty jar with my finger. Seven days of hiding at the cabin had depleted everything except my determination to avoid Copper Ridge.

I stood at the kitchen counter, staring into Dorothy's empty refrigerator. The shelves gleamed back at me, spotless and accusing. A cramp seized my stomach, a familiar twist of hunger and dread. The empty refrigerator wasn't just an inconvenience; it was an eviction notice from my sanctuary.

Patterson's General Store waited at the end of a twenty-minute drive. Twenty minutes to town. Five minutes to grab essentials. Twenty minutes back. I could manage forty-five minutes of exposure.

The keys felt cold in my hand as I locked the cabin door behind me. My SUV started on the second try, the engine protesting the mountain morning. I reversed down the dirt driveway, tires crunching over pine needles, and turned onto Forest Road 247.

The switchbacks down the mountain felt like a countdown. Each curve tightened the knot in my stomach, pulling me closer to Main Street and the whispers I knew were waiting. My grip on the steering wheel was so tight my knuckles ached, the leather creaking with each hairpin turn.

Copper Ridge spread below me in the valley—red brick fire station, church steeple, rows of storefronts that hadn't changed since the mining days. Smoke rose from chimneys despite the June warmth. The mountains pressed in on all sides, beautiful and suffocating.

I parked outside Patterson's, choosing a spot near the edge of the lot where I could make a quick escape if needed. Through the store's front window, I spotted Ed Patterson behind the register, his gray head bent over something.

Deep breath. Shoulders back. Face neutral.

The bell above the door announced my arrival with a cheerful chime that felt like a fire alarm. Ed's head snapped up. His eyes found me over his wire-rimmed glasses, recognition flashing across his weathered face.

"Well, hello there." He straightened, setting down his pencil. "Miss Reed, right? Staying up at the Clairmore place?"

"That's right." I grabbed a basket from the stack by the door, the plastic handle already slick in my palm.

"Settling in okay? That road can be tricky after rain."

"It's fine. Thank you."

I turned toward the produce section before he could ask anything else. The store stretched narrow and deep, aisles packed tight with everything from canned beans to fishing lures. The buzz of the fluorescent lights drilled into my skull. Everything was cast in a harsh, clinical white that felt like being under interrogation.

Two women stood by the dairy case, their heads bent together. The town gossips. Every story needs them. I just hated being their new main character. Their voices carried despite the attempted whispers.

"—never seen anything like it. Right there at the engagement party—"

"—Poor Mason and Lily. Their special night—"

"—something about Portland? Five years ago—"

My feet froze to the linoleum. The basket handle cut into my palm.

"— Wyatt Drake of all people. You know he never stays—"

"—looked ready to combust. Both of them—"

"—wonder what really happened—"

Heat flooded my cheeks, a hot, shameful tide. I knew this narrative. God, I'd helped craft a hundred versions of it in marketing meetings—the mysterious woman from out of town, the local hero with a past, the explosive reunion that everyone whispers about. I'd sold these tropes to readers for years, packaged them in glossy covers with promises of happy endings.

But standing here, cast as the other woman in a story I hadn't written, the irony tasted like ash. They didn't know about Brandon. Didn't know I'd been the one with secrets, the one who'd cheated, even if only for a weekend. In their version, I was probably the temptress who'd seduced poor Wyatt Drake away from his wandering ways.

The worst part? I couldn't even correct them. Because explaining would make it worse. Would make me what they already suspected—someone who didn't belong here, who'd brought city complications to their simple mountain town.

I'd spent my career analyzing reader reactions to romantic conflict. Now I was living it, and every whispered word felt like a one-star review I couldn't respond to.

My fingers fumbled, grabbing the first box they touched—granola, maybe?—and I fled toward the bread aisle, their whispers chasing me like wasps. The women glanced my way, their conversation dying mid-sentence. One nudged the other. They both offered bright, fake smiles before hurrying toward the front of the store.

The bread aisle offered three choices: white, wheat, or a dense-looking loaf labeled "mountain grain" that could probably stop a bullet. I reached for the wheat.

"Finding everything?" Ed Patterson materialized at my elbow, his worn boots making no sound on the creaking floorboards.

I managed not to jump. "Yes, thanks."

"You know, my wife makes fresh bread on Tuesdays. Sells it here. Much better than the packaged stuff." His eyes glinted behind his glasses, studying me like I was a puzzle missing pieces. "Heard that party was quite the shindig. Lily and Mason, they make a fine couple. It's good to see all the Drake boys settling down. Well, most of 'em."

"I've been working. The cabin's perfect for writing."

"Ah yes, Lily mentioned you're an author. What kind of books?"

"Fiction." I moved past him toward the refrigerated section. He followed.

"Romance, right? My wife loves those. Always reading about firefighters and such." His tone stayed conversational, but the emphasis on "firefighters" wasn't subtle.

The eggs were right there. I just had to grab a carton, add milk and coffee to my basket, and escape. My hand reached for the eggs.

The bell chimed. I knew without looking that my forty-five-minute plan had just imploded.

"Emma!" Lily's voice sliced through the hum of the coolers, and the tension in my shoulders eased a fraction. A friendly face. A life raft.

She appeared around the endcap, dressed in her work clothes—khakis and a polo with the Colorado Fire Inspector logo embroidered on the chest. Her engagement ring caught the light as she reached for my arm.

"I was hoping I'd run into you." Her eyes swept over my basket, taking in the meager supplies, the tension in my shoulders. "Actually, that's a lie. I drove by and saw your car. Come on."

She steered me toward the door with the efficiency of someone used to evacuating buildings. Ed Patterson watched us leave, disappointment clear on his face.

Outside, the morning sun hit my face like a slap. Lily guided me to my car, positioning us so our backs were to the store windows.

"You okay?" Her hand stayed on my arm, warm and steadying.

"Fine. Just needed supplies."

"Emma." The word carried gentle reproach. "The whole town's been talking about the party. What's going on between you and Wyatt? I didn't even know you knew each other."

"It's not your fault." I stopped, reorganized. "We're adults. It was just unexpected."

A skeptical arch of her brow told me she wasn't buying it. She glanced around, confirming we were alone, then leaned closer.

"He's been taking every out-of-town assignment Mason offers. Haven't seen him in a week."

The words landed like stones in my chest, and my brain immediately split into warring factions.

See? I was right. I was always right. This is what he does—runs the moment things get complicated. He couldn't even last a week in the same town as me before fleeing to Helena or wherever the hell he was going. This is who he is. This is who he's always been.

But underneath the vindication, something sharper twisted. He wasn't even trying. Hadn't sent a text, hadn't shown up at the cabin, hadn't made any attempt to fight for... what? For us? There was no us. There never had been, not really. Just three days five years ago and one explosive encounter at an engagement party. I walked away from him.

So why did it hurt that he'd given up so easily?

And then—relief. Sweet, shameful relief flooding through me like anesthesia. I wouldn't have to see him at the grocery store, wouldn't have to navigate awkward encounters on Main Street, wouldn't have to feel my heart jackrabbit every time a truck that might be his drove past the cabin. I could go back to my sanctuary, my manuscript, my carefully constructed solitude.

The tension I'd been carrying for seven days eased, just slightly. No confrontation meant no risk of saying something I couldn't take back. No risk of wanting something I couldn't have.

I was safe again. Alone, but safe.

She pulled her phone from her pocket, swiped to her calendar. "Speaking of which, we need to talk about wedding details."

My stomach dropped. "Sure."

"The wedding's in late August. That's less than three months to order dresses, get alterations, plan the bachelorette party—" She paused, reading the blank panic on my face.

Her voice softened. "Emma, if this is too complicated with Wyatt being Mason's best man—"

"It's not complicated." The lie tasted sour. "We can be professional."

"Professional." She repeated the word like she was testing its weight. "You realize you'll be walking down the aisle together after the vows?

Standing across from each other during the ceremony? The reception dance?"

Each scenario played out in vivid, agonizing detail—Wyatt's arm linked with mine, the scent of his cologne, his hand settling on the small of my back during the first dance. Hours of forced proximity while everyone watched, remembered, and whispered about the night our past had detonated in public.

"I can handle it."

"I could talk to Mason. Maybe—"

"No." The word came out harder than intended. I softened my voice. "Lily, this is your wedding. We can manage a few hours of politeness."

She looked skeptical but didn't argue. "If you're sure."

"I'm sure."

"Okay." She squeezed my arm. "But if you need to talk, or if things get weird—"

"I'll be fine. Really. I just need to focus on my book, help with your wedding, and then—" I caught myself before saying "escape to Seattle."

"And then what?"

"Just... see what happens."

Lily's expression suggested she heard everything I hadn't said. "Three months is a long time, Em."

"Or not long enough." The words slipped out before I could stop them.

She pulled me into a hug that smelled like her vanilla perfume mixed with something sharp—probably whatever chemicals fire inspectors used.

"He's taking the Helena job next week," she whispered against my ear. "Two-week assignment. Mason told me this morning."

I pulled back. "I didn't ask—"

"I know." She smiled, sad and knowing. "But I thought you should know."

She left me standing by my car, groceries forgotten in the basket I'd abandoned inside. Two weeks. He'd be gone two more weeks. That should have felt like relief. Instead, it felt like confirmation—we were both so desperate to avoid each other that he was fleeing the state.

I went back inside, ignored Ed Patterson's eager expression, paid for my pathetic collection of supplies, and drove back to the cabin on autopilot. The mountain road blurred. Not from tears. Just from the bright morning sun.

The cabin welcomed me back with its familiar silence. Back in the cabin's silence, I unpacked. The carton of eggs felt cold and fragile in my hands. I placed it in the refrigerator door, the small click of the plastic loud in the quiet kitchen. Bread on the counter. Coffee in the cabinet. Each item finding its place, a small act of order against the chaos churning in my gut.

Walking down an aisle with Wyatt's arm through mine. Standing at the altar while Mason and Lily exchanged vows about forever. Dancing while the whole town watched and whispered.

Three months. Late August. Less than ninety days to pretend Wyatt Drake didn't affect me. To smile for photos and make toasts about true love while standing next to the only man who'd ever made me believe in it.

The mountains filled my window, unchanging and eternal. Somewhere beyond them, Wyatt was packing for Helena. Running. Just like I'd run five years ago.

We were so good at leaving. Neither of us had figured out how to stay.

I set my fingers on the keys but couldn't make them move. The blank space after Chapter 15 stretched like the summer ahead—full of possibility and dread in equal measure.

The cursor blinked. Waited. Just like everything else in this too-quiet cabin where Dorothy's love story haunted every corner and mine couldn't even make it onto the page.

The Best Man's Burden

Wyatt

The church door weighed more than a fire axe. I stood on the worn stone steps, hand on the iron handle, watching my reflection warp in the old glass. Three months. That's how long I'd lasted. Three months of bouncing between fire assignments, and running from the one person I wanted to run to. Three months of not seeing her.

Inside, voices echoed off wood and stone. Mason's laugh. Lily's bright instructions. The pastor's patient tone.

And somewhere in there, Emma.

I pulled the door open.

The sanctuary stretched before me—rows of oak pews scarred by decades of weddings and funerals, stained glass throwing patches of ruby and amber across the floor. The place smelled like my childhood:

lemon polish and old hymnals, that particular dust that collects in sacred spaces.

"There he is." Mason stood at the altar in jeans and a polo, arms crossed, the corner of his mouth hitched in that way that said he had opinions. A lot of them. "Starting to think you'd bailed."

"Traffic."

"From where? Your apartment's five minutes away."

I walked down the aisle, boots loud on the hardwood.

Every step felt wrong. I was an imposter in this place, surrounded by the architecture of commitment, here to celebrate the one thing I'd spent my entire life running from. Mason stood at that altar like he'd been born to it—solid, certain, ready to promise forever without flinching. Meanwhile, my insides were a wildfire, all chaos and smoke, no clear line to cut. I looked at my brother and felt it all at once: admiration for his courage, and a suffocating terror that this life—this settled, rooted, forever kind of life—could swallow me whole. The same way I'd always believed it had swallowed him, though looking at him now, he didn't look swallowed. He looked... whole. And that scared me even more.

The wedding party clustered near the altar—Javi and Luke in matching confusion about where to stand, Madison directing them with pregnant authority, James leaning against a pew with his usual easy calm.

Then movement to my left. A flash of yellow.

Emma.

A yellow sundress that hit me like a gut punch. Bare shoulders. Hair falling loose, catching the light. Three months I'd spent trying to burn that image out of my head, and here she was. Real. Worse than I remembered. Better.

She glanced up from her conversation with Lily. Our eyes met for half a second before she turned away, sudden interest in the order of service in her hand.

"Wyatt." Lily's voice cut through the noise. "Perfect timing. We're about to run through the processional."

Pastor Williams, ancient and patient, gathered us at the back of the church. "Simple enough, folks. Processional, vows, recessional. We'll walk through it twice, make sure everyone knows their positions."

He started pairing people off. Javi with Madison. Luke with one of Lily's Denver friends.

"Wyatt and Emma, you're first after the happy couple."

Emma's shoulders went rigid. I moved to stand beside her, careful to leave space between us. Close enough to catch her scent—something light and floral that hadn't changed. Close enough to see the sun freckles across her nose that hadn't been there in May.

"You'll proceed together," Pastor Williams demonstrated, "lady's hand through the gentleman's arm, traditional style."

Emma slipped her hand through my offered arm like she was handling live explosives. The contact shot straight through my shirt. Her fingers lightly touched the fabric, her body angled away even as we stood connected.

"Good, good. Now, steady pace. This isn't a race."

The pianist launched into something classical. We walked. Emma's hand on my arm weighed nothing and everything. Each step measured, controlled. Her breathing deliberately even. Mine had gone shallow the moment she'd touched me.

Halfway down the aisle, I couldn't stand the silence. "Emma, can we—"

"Not now." Her voice sharp. "This is Lily's weekend."

"I just want to—"

"I said not now." She stared straight ahead. Her jaw was set, a stubborn line I knew all too well. A tiny muscle jumped near her ear. She was holding on by a thread. But I caught the tell—the way she pressed her lips together, fighting for control.

We reached the back of the church. Her hand was gone. Not just released—retracted, like she'd touched a live wire. The space between us stretched wider than the church.

Pastor Williams walked us through the ceremony positions. Where to stand. When to move. How to hold the bouquets and rings. Professional. Mechanical. Emma never looked at me directly, her attention fixed on Lily or the pastor or the stained glass behind my head.

"Let's run it once more," Pastor Williams announced. "From the top."

Back to the altar. Back to that careful touch, her hand through my arm. The second run hurt worse—now I knew exactly how little pressure she'd use, just how far she'd lean away.

This time I kept my mouth shut. Counted the steps. Sixteen from door to altar. Sixteen chances to memorize how she felt beside me.

Pastor Williams clapped his hands together, his face crinkling into a thousand happy lines. "Beautiful. Tomorrow will be perfect."

Emma escaped to Lily's side immediately, diving into discussion about bouquet angles. I stood with the groomsmen, half-listening to Javi's story about his kids, watching her laugh at something Madison said. The sound hit dead center in my chest.

"You good?" Mason appeared at my shoulder.

"Fine."

"Sure you are." He clapped my back. "Come on. Dinner's at the Grizzly."

The bar had transformed for the rehearsal dinner. Tables pushed together to form one long surface, white tablecloths attempting dignity over scarred wood. Tea lights in mason jars, because Lily had insisted on "rustic charm." The smell of barbecue competed with beer and perfume.

The seating arrangement was Lily's work—diplomatic and careful. Mason and Lily at the center. Parents and family radiating out. Emma at one end, me at the other. Maximum distance while maintaining the fiction of celebration.

Mac dropped into the chair beside me, already working on a beer. "So that was comfortable to watch."

"Drop it."

"Just saying, you two looked like you were handling dynamite."

"Mac—"

"Whatever you did, fix it. That was painful to watch."

"Who says I did something? She's the one who left without warning."

The food came out—platters of ribs and brisket, cornbread and coleslaw. Conversation flowed around me. Mac telling stories about our worst fires, getting Luke wide-eyed about smoke jumping. Someone's kid crying in the corner. The clink of glasses and silverware.

I couldn't focus on any of it.

Emma sat between Lily and one of the Denver friends, picking at her food. She'd pinned her hair up since the church, exposing the curve of her neck. Every time she laughed, my head turned. An instinct, like a spotter plane homing in on a smoke plume.

She caught me looking once. Our eyes held for a breath before she turned to Madison, asking something about pregnancy that got them deep in conversation.

The toasts started with Lily's father—something about little girls growing up and finding good men. Then Mason's turn, thanking everyone for coming, for being part of their story.

"Wyatt." Mason raised his beer toward me. "Your turn, best man."

I stood, the chair scraping loud. Sixty faces turned toward me. Emma studied her water glass.

"Mason." The words felt thick. "My brother. The one who stayed. Who built something real here in Copper Ridge. Who fought for what mattered."

My throat went dry. I lifted my beer.

"Tomorrow you're marrying Lily, and everyone here knows you're getting the better deal." Laughter rippled through the crowd. "But what you might not know is how you changed her too. Lily came here looking for violations, for problems to solve. Instead, she found home. Found you."

I risked a glance at Emma. She was watching me now, something unreadable in her expression.

"Love's not about perfect timing or easy choices. It's about choosing each other even when it's hard. About staying when every instinct says run."

Stay. The word hammered in my chest, every syllable aimed at Emma like I could will her to hear what I couldn't say out loud. Just stay. Let me prove I can be the man who chooses you, even if every instinct I have is screaming to run for the state line. Even if my hands are shaking and my throat's closing and I can feel the old panic clawing at my ribs. These words—choosing, staying—I'm testing them like a rope before a rappel, trying to convince myself as much as her that they can hold weight. That I can hold.

"Mason and Lily, you figured that out."

I raised my glass higher. "To Mason and Lily. To choosing each other. To staying."

The crowd echoed the toast. Glasses clinked. Emma's eyes met mine across the length of the table. The look in them wasn't forgiveness.

It wasn't anger. It was... recognition. She'd heard every word I hadn't said. She knew that toast wasn't for Mason. It was for her. For us.

Then she looked away, and the moment shattered.

The dinner wound down. People started filtering out, hugging the bride and groom, making promises about tomorrow. I helped Mac find his hotel, and did the duties required of the best man.

When I finally got free, Emma was already in the parking lot, keys in hand, almost to her car.

"Emma, wait—"

But she was already sliding behind the wheel. The engine turned over. Headlights swept across me as she reversed, then she was gone, taillights disappearing down Main Street.

I stood in the empty parking lot, the mountains black shapes against the stars. Tomorrow she'd stand across from me while Mason and Lily promised forever. Walk down that aisle on my arm again.

Mac was wrong. Some things couldn't be fixed.

Some things just had to be survived.

Vows in Blue Silk

♥

Wyatt

The church smelled like my father's funeral.

I stood at the altar, Mac beside me, watching Copper Ridge file through the doors. Same dust motes dancing in colored light from the stained glass. Same weight in my chest, though today it came from different grief entirely.

"You're gonna crack a tooth." Mac adjusted his tie, voice low enough that Mason wouldn't hear from his position by the vestry door.

My jaw unclenched. The rented suit pulled across my shoulders. I rolled them back, but the tension stayed put. It had been my shadow since four this morning, when I'd woken up staring at the ceiling, counting all the reasons this was a terrible idea.

"Brother, you need to breathe before you pass out and ruin your brother's wedding."

"I'm breathing."

"Sure you are." Mac's hand landed on my shoulder, solid and grounding. "She's just a woman."

Just a woman. Right. Just the only woman who'd ever made me want to stop running. Just the woman I'd spent five years trying to forget while jumping out of planes into wildfires. Just the woman who'd be walking toward me in approximately five minutes wearing a dress that would burn through what was left of my composure.

The organ wheezed to life, sending Bach through the rafters. Mrs. Henderson had been playing weddings here since before I was born, her fingers finding the keys through muscle memory alone. The congregation stood in a rustle of fabric and whispered anticipation.

Mason appeared at the altar, taking his position. His hands were steady. Of course they were. Mason had never doubted anything in his life. He'd rebuilt Dad's cabin with his bare hands, saved the fire station from closure, and convinced a by-the-book inspector to stay in a town with one traffic light.

"You good?" His voice carried that older-brother concern that still made me feel fifteen years old.

"Why does everyone keep asking me that?"

The corner of his mouth twitched. "Because you look like you're about to bolt."

The processional music shifted to something lighter. Madison was first. Her pregnancy showed now, rounding her in that way that made James's face go soft every time he looked at her. She moved down the aisle with practiced ease, glowing with that particular contentment that came from knowing where you belonged.

Next was Lily's friend from Denver—Sarah or Sandra or something that started with S.

Then the music paused. That heartbeat of silence before everything changed.

Emma appeared in the doorway, and the air left my lungs like I'd walked into a backdraft. A sudden, total vacuum.

This wasn't just beauty. This was everything I couldn't have, wrapped in blue silk and walking toward an altar. Home. The word slammed into me with physical force. She was home—the kind I'd spent five years chasing fires to avoid thinking about. The kind that meant roots and staying and all the things that terrified me more than any wildfire ever could. My chest constricted. Every instinct screamed at me to run, to bolt out the side door before she got any closer, before that image of her walking toward me—not away, toward—burned itself permanently into my brain. But my feet stayed planted. Anchored. Just like she would anchor me if I let her.

The soft blue dress moved like water, skimming her curves in a way that should have been illegal in a church. Her hair was up, exposing the long line of her neck, the delicate spot behind her ear where she'd dabbed perfume. Afternoon light caught the auburn highlights I'd forgotten about, turning them to copper fire.

She lifted her chin, that stubborn angle I knew meant she was gathering courage, and started down the aisle alone. Her fingers gripped the bouquet—white roses and something purple—tight enough to strangle the stems. Her gaze fixed on a point over the pastor's head and a small smile graced her lips, clearly forced. She wouldn't look at me. I could see the effort it took in the stubborn set of her jaw.

The distance between us collapsed with each step. Twenty feet. Fifteen. Ten.

She reached the altar and took her position across from me. The air in the space between us felt thick, charged, like the moments before a lightning strike. Her chest rose and fell in careful rhythm. Controlled. Measured. Fighting for the same composure that was slipping through my fingers like smoke.

The music swelled into the traditional wedding march. The congregation turned. Lily appeared, veiled and luminous, her father beside her looking like he might cry.

Mason made a sound beside me—soft, private, meant for no one else. His whole face transformed, years of weight lifting from his shoulders as his bride walked toward him. This was what certainty looked like.

My gaze was dragged back to Emma. She watched Lily, her lips parted, her expression unguarded and raw. Her throat moved as she swallowed hard, and I wanted to cross the space between us. Wanted to pull her against me and whisper that we could have this too.

Pastor Williams began the ceremony, his voice rolling through the familiar words about love and commitment, about two becoming one. I tried to focus on my brother. On my duty as best man. On anything except the way Emma's skin glowed in the colored light, the way she bit her lower lip when she was trying not to cry.

"Mason and Lily have written their own vows," Pastor Williams announced, stepping back.

Mason pulled a folded paper from his pocket. His hands were still steady. "Lily." Her name came out rough with emotion. "Six months ago, you walked into my station ready to shut us down. You had your clipboard and your regulations and those ridiculous heels."

Soft laughter rippled through the church. Lily's smile bloomed behind her veil.

"You challenged everything I thought I knew about safety, about rules, about what mattered. But more than that, you challenged what I thought I knew about myself. About what I deserved." Mason's voice dropped, intimate despite the crowd. "I spent years thinking my life was the station, that duty meant sacrifice. You taught me that wasn't living. That was just existing."

The words hit like falling timber. Duty meant sacrifice. That was just existing. Each sentence was a mirror held up to my own face, reflecting back five years of cowardice I'd dressed up as honor. I'd told myself the smokejumping was necessary. That someone had to do it. That I was serving something bigger than myself. But Mason was right—that wasn't living. That was running. I'd been running since the day I left Emma in Portland, running from the terrifying possibility that she could be my home. That I could choose her and build something real instead of jumping into fires because at least there I knew what I was fighting.

"I choose you, Lily Zhang. Not because it's easy or convenient or practical. I choose you because you're my home. The place I want to return to every night. The person I want to wake up next to every morning. I choose you today, tomorrow, and every day after that. Even when it's hard. Especially when it's hard. Because that's what love is."

The church had gone silent except for someone crying softly in the back rows. My throat burned. Beside me, Mac shifted his weight, and I knew without looking that he was thinking about his own ghosts.

Lily's turn. She didn't need paper. Her voice rang clear and certain through the space.

"Mason Drake, you terrified me. Not because you were mean or difficult, but because you saw through every wall I'd built. You saw the frightened woman hiding behind regulations and inspection reports. The woman who'd been running for two years, convinced that feeling nothing was better than risking pain."

Emma's breathing had gone shallow. I watched her chest rise and fall in quick, small movements.

"You didn't let me run. You stood there, solid as the mountains, and showed me what bravery really looked like. Not the absence of fear, but choosing love despite it. Choosing to build something together despite knowing it could all burn down."

My throat closed. I couldn't look away from Emma. Her profile was backlit by colored light, and I could see her swallow hard, see the way her fingers trembled on the bouquet. Choosing love despite fear. Not running. Every word was an indictment. I was the coward here. I'd run from Emma because what I felt for her was too big, too consuming, too permanent. She represented everything I'd told myself I couldn't have—stability, home, a future that didn't involve jumping out of planes to outrun my own heart. I looked at her now and saw that same potential Mason was claiming with Lily. That life-altering, soul-deep love that would change everything. And it terrified me. God, it terrified me. But standing here, watching my brother choose courage, I realized something worse: losing her terrified me more.

My hand twitched. I wanted to reach across the space. Wanted to grab Emma and make her understand that every word Lily spoke was about us too.

"I choose you, Mason. I choose this town, this life, this family. I choose to start building. With you. Always with you."

Pastor Williams called for the rings. I fumbled in my pocket, the simple gold bands catching the light as I passed them over. Mason's fingers brushed mine, steady and sure.

"Do you, Mason, take Lily to be your wedded wife?"

"I do." No hesitation. No doubt.

"Do you, Lily, take Mason to be your wedded husband?"

"I do." The words rang like a bell, clear and true.

"You may kiss the bride."

Mason lifted Lily's veil with the kind of reverence typically reserved for sacred things. Their kiss was everything a wedding kiss should be—tender and claiming, a promise and a seal.

The church erupted in applause. Mrs. Henderson launched into the recessional with enthusiasm that made the organ wheeze in protest.

Mason and Lily started back up the aisle, joy radiating from them in waves.

Our turn.

Emma crossed to me, her movements careful and precise. She slipped her hand through my offered arm. The contact was a jolt, a live current against the fabric of my suit that went straight to my bones. Her fingers barely touched the fabric of my suit, her body angled away even as we moved together. I put my hand over her hand and looked at her with what I hoped was an offer of a truce. She didn't pull away.

Physical memory flooded through me—her body against mine in that Portland hotel room, the catch of her breath when I'd kissed behind her ear, the way she'd whispered my name like a prayer. I wanted to pull her close right here in front of everyone. Wanted to stop walking and turn her to face me and confess everything—that she was the only reason I'd stayed in Copper Ridge, that every fire I'd jumped had been an attempt to burn her out of my system, that it hadn't worked. That nothing worked. But she held herself so rigidly, so carefully distant even as we moved together, and I didn't know how to bridge that gap. How do I say it? The question repeated with each step. How do I tell her she's the only reason I'm still here, the only thing that matters, when I can see she's already got one foot out the door?

We walked. The aisle stretched forever. Every face we passed was watching—Rita from the diner dabbing her eyes, Ed from the general store grinning like he'd won the lottery, Ruby from the salon already whispering to her seatmate.

Emma's perfume wrapped around me. Something floral with an undertone of vanilla that made me think of the three days in Portland when everything had been possible. Her hand trembled against my arm. I wanted to still that tremor. Wanted to never let go.

We made it outside into the afternoon sun. Emma's hand disappeared from my arm the instant we cleared the church doors, and she moved away like she'd been released from a trap.

"Photo time!" The photographer—someone's cousin from Denver—started arranging the wedding party against the church's white clapboard.

"Wyatt, Emma, closer together please."

Emma stepped toward me, careful to maintain inches between us. The photographer frowned.

"Closer. You're in the wedding party, not strangers."

Emma moved again. Still not close enough for the photographer, who actually walked over and physically pushed us together. Emma's shoulder pressed against my chest. The heat of her body burned through both our clothes. I wrapped my arm around her waist and pulled her closer.

"Perfect! Now smile!"

We smiled. Held it while the camera clicked. Smiled through the full wedding party shots, the guys-only shots, the girls-only shots. My face ached from the effort of looking happy while Emma stood close enough to touch but might as well have been on the moon.

Finally, mercifully, the photographer released us. "Reception photos later!"

Emma vanished into the crowd of guests heading for their cars. I watched her go, that blue dress disappearing behind SUVs and pickup trucks.

"You know," Mac appeared beside me, "you could try talking to her instead of staring like a lovesick teenager."

"She doesn't want to talk to me."

"Have you tried?"

"Last night—"

"Running after her in a parking lot doesn't count." Mac straightened his tie. "Come on. Open bar at the reception. You look like you need it."

The fire station didn't smell like itself. The usual scent of diesel and rubber was buried under barbecue and Lily's roses. Where Engine One usually sat, round tables covered in white linens waited for guests. String lights crisscrossed overhead, turning the industrial bay into something almost magical.

The head table stretched across the front, elevated on a small platform. Place cards in Lily's neat handwriting told the story—Mason and Lily in the center, wedding party radiating out. Emma on Lily's side. Me on Mason's. Close enough to pass the salt.

"Ladies and gentlemen," Javi had appointed himself MC, standing with a microphone that squealed feedback. "Please welcome Mr. and Mrs. Drake!"

Mason and Lily entered to thunderous applause. They looked like they'd been married for years already, that particular ease that came from being with who you belonged with.

Dinner was pulled pork and brisket, Colorado comfort food. I pushed food around my plate, hyperaware of Emma three seats away. She'd pinned a loose curl back, exposing more of her neck. Every time she laughed at something Lily said, the sound went straight through me.

"How's the book going?" Lily's question carried clearly over the dinner noise.

Emma's shoulders tightened. "It's... progressing."

"Still stuck on the ending?"

"The characters won't cooperate." Emma's voice carried forced lightness. "They keep circling the same conflict."

Someone clinked a glass, saving us from further conversation. The speeches started—James talking about brothers and family, Javi telling embarrassing stories from Mason's rookie days, Mac standing to say something about Mason being the kind of leader men would follow into any fire.

Then the music started. "First dance for the bride and groom!"

Mason led Lily onto the cleared floor, and they swayed to something slow and country. The whole room watched them, but they only saw each other.

"Wedding party, join them!"

My stomach dropped. I stood, walked around the table to where Emma sat frozen.

"We don't have to—" she started.

"Yeah, we do." I extended my hand. "One dance. We can manage one dance."

She stared at my hand like it might bite. Then, slowly, she placed hers in mine and let me lead her onto the floor.

The appropriate position for this kind of dance was clear—one hand on her waist, the other holding hers. The instant my palm settled against the curve of her hip, a low hum started under my skin. A circuit completed. She was warm through the thin fabric, her body remembering mine even as she held herself stiff and distant.

"Relax." The word came out rougher than intended. "People are watching."

"I am relaxed."

"You're about as relaxed as a fence post."

She shifted, letting herself move with the music instead of against it. The adjustment brought her closer, her chest almost brushing mine. Her perfume filled the space between us.

"You look beautiful." The words were out before I could haul them back.

Her fingers tightened on my shoulder. "Don't."

"It's just an observation."

"It's not *just* anything with you."

We turned with the music, and her body followed mine like it had been programmed to, that perfect synchronization that had always existed between us.

"Is it hard?" The question came out low, meant only for her. "Being near me?"

She lifted her eyes to mine for the first time all day. "Yes. Obviously."

"Good." My hand pressed lightly at her waist, pulling her imperceptibly closer. "At least I'm not the only one suffering."

"Wyatt—"

"Three months, Emma. Three months of wondering why you won't talk to me, why you're avoiding me. Three months of—"

"You think it's been easy for me?" Her voice cracked. "You think I haven't spent every day since we met trying to forget you?"

"Have you?"

"Have I what?"

"Forgotten."

The song ended. Another started immediately, but Emma pulled away, stepping back like I'd burned her.

"I need air."

She walked off the dance floor, heading for the bay doors that opened onto the back lot. I watched her go, that blue dress disappearing into the evening shadows beyond the lights.

Mac appeared at my elbow. "Go after her."

"She said she needed air."

"She needs you to stop being an idiot." He pushed me toward the doors. "Go. Before you lose her for another five years."

The Exit Strategy

Wyatt

The evening air hit my face like cold water, sharp with pine and the promise of fall coming early to the mountains. I pushed through the back door of the fire station, the metal handle rough against my palm. Behind me, the wedding reception continued—laughter and music bleeding through the walls, the bass line of some country song vibrating through the concrete under my feet.

Emma stood twenty feet away, her back to me, arms wrapped tight around herself like she could hold all her pieces together through sheer force. The security light above cast her in harsh white, turning the blue of her dress to something closer to gray. Her shoulders rose and fell with each breath, too fast, too shallow.

"Emma."

Her spine went rigid. She didn't turn.

I stepped closer, gravel crunching under my dress shoes. The sound was too loud in the quiet. "We need to talk."

"No." Her voice came out flat, careful. "We don't."

"Three months of avoiding each other isn't working."

She laughed, but there was no humor in it. "Seems to be working fine."

"You call this fine?" I moved closer, close enough to catch her perfume mixing with the smell of barbecue smoke from the reception. "Dancing around each other like strangers? Pretending those three days in Portland never happened?"

She finally turned. The security light threw shadows across her face, made the green of her eyes look black. "There's nothing to talk about, Wyatt. Portland was a mistake. Let's leave it at that."

The word hit me in the chest. "A mistake? Is that what it was to you? Because it sure as hell wasn't a mistake to me."

She looked away, toward the mountains invisible in the darkness. "Lily mentioned you're staying in town longer than usual."

The subject change threw me. "Mason needs help with some projects."

"And then?"

"And then what?"

"And then you leave." She said it like a fact. "It's what you do."

"How did you—"

"Small town. Everyone knows everything." Her arms tightened around herself.

"I heard you extended your rental." I watched her face for any reaction. "Through December."

Her jaw tightened. "Just to finish my book."

"And then?"

She met my eyes, chin lifting. "Then back to Seattle. My real life."

Real life. Like everything here—the mountains, the town, me—was just some fantasy she'd wandered into by accident. "That's your real life? Seattle?"

"As opposed to what?"

"You're the one who ran out on me."

"I had my reasons."

"What would you call leaving without a word? Because I woke up and you were just—gone."

"I'd call it complicated."

"Everything's complicated with you."

"What's that supposed to mean?"

She turned to face me fully, and the anger in her eyes was better than the careful nothing from before. "It means I panicked, okay? It means I got scared of how much I wanted to stay."

That small admission nearly had me reaching for her. I closed my eyes and took a deep breath.

"I came home for my brother's wedding. You're here, someone I never thought I would see again. I would like another chance for us, and I'm staying for a while."

"For how long?" The question hung between us like smoke. "Until the next fire? The next adventure? The next reason to run?"

"I don't run."

"That's all you do." Her voice cracked on the words. "Oregon, California, Montana, Alaska—"

"That's my job."

"That's your excuse." She took a step toward me, then caught herself, stepped back again. "What do you expect, Wyatt? That I'd wait here? That I'd put my life on hold hoping you'd—"

She bit off the words, but I heard them. Hoping I'd decide to stay. That's why she ran, because she thought I would never settle down. At the time, it was true, but not so much anymore. I wasn't sure how to tell her that.

"Emma—"

"No." She shook her head, backing toward the door. "I'm done with this conversation."

"We haven't even started this conversation."

"We had it five years ago. We had it in Portland when you told me about the Alaska job you'd already accepted." She reached for the door handle. "You're not permanent, Wyatt. You never have been. I left before you left me."

"I want to try with you, Emma. We can try together and see if it works."

She froze, hand on the door. For a second, I thought she might turn around. Then she pulled the door open, wedding music spilling out into the night. "Wanting and doing are two different things."

The door closed behind her with a soft click that sounded final.

I stood there in the dark, her words echoing in my head. You're not permanent. You never have been.

The sound of footsteps on gravel made me turn. Mason stood there, tie loosened, suit jacket gone. He'd lost the boutonniere somewhere, and his hair stuck up where he'd been running his hands through it—a gesture I recognized from our childhood, from every time he'd had to be the adult when he was barely more than a kid himself.

"Shouldn't you be inside?" My voice came out rough. "It's your wedding."

"Lily sent me." He moved to lean against the wall beside me.

"I'm fine."

"You're an idiot."

I didn't argue. Couldn't, really.

"She's right, you know." Mason pulled out his flask—the one that had been our father's—and took a sip before passing it to me. Whiskey, smooth and burning. "You do run."

Easy for him to say. He'd never had to leave. "It's my job."

"No, your job is fighting fires. Running is what you do to avoid fighting the ones that matter."

I took another pull from the flask, the burn giving me something to focus on besides his words. "You don't know what you're talking about. Spare me the big brother wisdom."

"Too bad. It's my wedding day. You have to listen." He took the flask back. "You know what your problem is?"

"I'm sure you're about to tell me."

"Your problem is you think leaving makes you free. But all it does is keep you from having anything worth staying for."

I wanted to argue. Wanted to tell him he was wrong, that my life meant something, that every fire I fought, every crew I led, every town I helped save—it all mattered. But the words stuck in my throat because underneath them was the truth I'd been avoiding: none of it had ever felt like enough.

"I used to think staying put was a sacrifice. After Dad died, I'll admit, some days it felt like I was losing myself to this town, to you kids. But I wasn't. I was choosing. There's a difference."

"You had to stay," I said, but even as the words left my mouth, they sounded hollow. "Someone had to take care of us."

"I could have left. Could have put you all in foster care, gone to college like I planned." Mason's voice was quiet, matter-of-fact. "Would've been easier, probably. But I chose you. Chose this town. Chose to build something that mattered."

The words hit harder than I wanted to admit. All these years, I'd told myself Mason had been trapped by circumstance, by duty. That I was different because I'd escaped. But he was right—he'd chosen. And I'd been running from having to choose anything at all.

"Mason—"

"I'm not saying it was easy. I'm not saying I didn't have days where I wanted to run. But staying isn't about sacrifice, Wyatt. It's about choosing something that matters more than the alternative."

"She's leaving anyway," I said, but the excuse felt weak even to my own ears. "What's the point?"

"So give her a reason to stay."

"I can't ask her to—"

"I'm not talking about asking." Mason turned to look at me. "You want her to believe you can be permanent? Stop telling her. Start showing her."

I opened my mouth to protest, to list all the reasons it wouldn't work, but Mason cut me off.

"You know what your real problem is? You've spent so long telling yourself that staying is settling, that commitment is a cage, that you can't see the truth right in front of you."

"What truth?"

"That you're already choosing her. You have been since Portland." He pushed off the wall. "The only question is whether you're going to keep lying to yourself about it."

He was right. I'd taken the Montana job, told myself it was what I wanted, but I'd delayed the start date. Extended my time in Copper Ridge. Found excuses to stay near a woman who'd made it clear she was leaving.

I'd been choosing her all along. I just hadn't had the guts to admit it.

"How?"

"That's for you to figure out." He pushed off the wall. "But maybe start by admitting that you came back to Copper Ridge this time for more than just helping with projects."

He headed for the door, then paused. "You know what Lily told me the night before she agreed to marry me? She said she'd spent two years running from fire, from feeling, from everything that mattered. Said she was done being afraid of getting burned."

"Emma's not Lily."

"No. But you're not as different from me as you think." He pulled open the door, music and light spilling out. "The question is whether you're brave enough to choose her, knowing she might leave anyway."

The door closed, leaving me alone with the darkness and the truth I'd been running from since the moment I saw Emma at my brother's engagement party.

I'd stayed in Copper Ridge longer than I'd planned because she was here.

And I had no idea what to do about it.

The mountains loomed invisible in the darkness, but I could feel them—the weight of all that stone and permanence. Inside, the wedding continued. People dancing, laughing, celebrating the choice two people had made to build something together.

Out here, I stood with empty hands and Emma's words still burning in my chest.

You're not permanent. You never have been.

Mason's words chased hers: There's a difference between asking and choosing.

I pulled out my phone, started to text Mac about the Montana job, about start dates and contracts. Then I stopped. Deleted the message.

Somewhere inside, Emma was probably avoiding the dance floor, finding excuses to be anywhere I wasn't. Her rental ran through December. Four months. Four months to prove I could choose something other than the next fire, the next escape, the next reason to run.

The door opened again. Luke stuck his head out. "Chief wants you for the toasts."

"Be right there."

Luke disappeared. I straightened my tie, ran a hand through my hair. Inside, I'd stand next to my brother and talk about commitment and love while Emma sat three seats away pretending we were strangers.

But Mason was right. I had to choose. And I was choosing her. Now I just had to figure out how to make her believe it.

The Waterfall Sanctuary

♥

Emma

The phone screen glowed against my palm in the pre-dawn darkness. Two messages from Wyatt, sent at 2:47 AM. So I wasn't the only one staring at the ceiling.

Can we talk?

I meant what I said. I want to try. I've stayed in Copper Ridge hoping we have a chance.

My thumb hovered over the delete button. The cabin's silence pressed against my eardrums, broken only by the tick of the wall clock and the settling of wood in the cooling night air. Outside, an owl called—low and mournful, the sound carrying across the valley.

Delete. Delete.

Gone. Like I'd never seen them. Like his words hadn't lodged themselves under my ribs where they burned with each breath.

I set the phone face-down on the nightstand and stared at the ceiling beams. Pine, aged to honey gold, solid as the mountains themselves. Everything here felt permanent. I pressed a hand to my stomach, the irony a hard, churning knot.

Coffee first. Always coffee first.

The kitchen floor chilled my bare feet as I padded to the counter. The coffee maker gurgled to life, filling the space with its familiar morning promise. Through the window, the first hint of dawn touched the peaks—purple bleeding into pink, the aspen groves below still pools of shadow. A few leaves had turned in the past week. Gold coins scattered among the green, autumn creeping in despite the calendar claiming we had days of summer left.

My laptop waited on the desk by the window, cursor blinking on Chapter Twenty. The same paragraph I'd been staring at for three days.

"You can't ask me to wait for you," Helena said, her back to the door. Outside, the sirens wailed—another fire, another emergency pulling Jake away. "Not when you're already gone."

That was it. That was where my fictional firefighter and his marketing specialist had stalled out, locked in an argument that felt too familiar to be fiction. Fifty thousand words of build-up, of tension and heat and connection, and I couldn't write them past this moment. Couldn't imagine how two people bridged that gap between wanting and staying.

"Come on," I muttered at the screen. "Just talk to each other."

But Helena and Jake remained frozen, suspended in that moment before everything either fell apart or came together. My fingers rested on the keys without typing.

Two days ago. Wyatt on my porch, morning sun catching the gold in his hair.

"Just a hike," he'd said. "The aspen trail. Two hours. You could use a break from that laptop."

I'd gripped the doorframe, using it as a barrier between us. "I have a deadline."

"Your deadline's not until December."

"How do you know that?"

His mouth quirked—not quite a smile. "Lily mentioned it."

Of course she had. My best friend the traitor.

"When are you leaving?" The question came out sharper than intended.

The light in his eyes dimmed. "That's not—I'm not going anywhere right now."

"Right now." I'd laughed, but it came out brittle. "So next week? Next month?"

"Emma—"

"I need to work." I'd stepped back, started to close the door. "The novel won't write itself."

The hurt that flashed across his face made my chest ache. But hurt was better than hope. Hope was dangerous. Hope made you believe in things like forever.

I shook off the memory and forced my fingers to move.

Jake stepped toward her. "What if I—"

What? What if he what? Promised to stay? Made declarations he couldn't keep?

Delete. Delete. Delete.

The blank space mocked me.

I shoved back from the desk. The chair hit the wall with a thud. My coffee was cold. The morning was gone. And I had nothing. Absolutely nothing.

"Need to move," I said to the empty cabin. "Need to think."

Twenty minutes later, I'd traded flannel for hiking clothes—moisture-wicking shirt, convertible pants, boots that had molded to my feet over three months of daily walks. The day pack held water, snacks, my notebook, and pepper spray that Lily insisted I carry despite never seeing anything more threatening than chipmunks.

The Aspen Trail—not the one Wyatt had suggested, definitely not—started a quarter mile from the cabin. I'd hiked it dozen of times, knew every switchback and stream crossing. My feet found the rhythm automatically while my mind wandered.

The forest wrapped around me, filtering the morning light through pine needles into something green and holy. A breeze stirred the branches overhead, sending a shower of golden aspen leaves spiraling down. They caught in my hair, crunched under my boots.

My phone buzzed in my pocket. I didn't check it.

The trail branched after the first mile—left toward the overlook, right toward the creek. My feet, moving on autopilot while my mind replayed Wyatt's hurt expression, took the path right. I didn't even notice the change until the sound of water grew louder, Crystal Creek running high despite the dry summer.

Another fork. I went left. Or thought I did.

The trees looked the same but different. Taller maybe, or closer together. The trail narrowed, less traveled. Grass grew across parts of it, suggesting few feet had passed this way recently.

I should turn back. Should retrace my steps to the last marker I recognized.

Instead, I pushed forward.

The sound came first—not just the creek but something bigger. A roar of water that vibrated through the ground. I followed it, leaving the trail entirely now, pushing through serviceberry bushes that caught at my clothes.

The trees opened suddenly. I stood at the edge of a pool, crystal clear and so blue it looked painted. Above it, a waterfall tumbled thirty feet down the cliff face, sending up a mist that caught the sun like shattered glass. The mist cooled my heated skin.

Behind the waterfall, darkness suggested depth.

A cave.

I worked my way around the pool's edge, boots slipping on wet rocks. The spray soaked through my shirt, raising goosebumps. The roar of water filled my ears, drowning thought.

The entrance was wider than it appeared from across the pool—tall enough to stand upright, wide enough for two people to walk side by side. Water curtained the opening, but there was a gap, a natural pathway that kept mostly dry.

I stepped through.

The temperature dropped ten degrees. The water's roar softened to a constant hush, like the ocean in a shell. My eyes adjusted slowly to the dimness, then widened.

The cave stretched back farther than expected, opening into a chamber the size of my cabin's living room. Mineral deposits hung from the ceiling—not quite stalactites but trying to be, centuries of patient dripping creating formations like frozen waterfalls. Some sections of the wall sparkled with crystalline deposits that caught and amplified the filtered light.

In the center of the chamber, a flat rock created a natural bench.

I sat, pulled out my notebook.

The words came without thought, my pen moving across paper like it had its own agenda.

They're both afraid. Helena won't wait because she's been left before—father, brother, first love. All of them choosing something else, somewhere else, someone else. Jake won't promise because promises feel like chains, and he watched his father die slowly from keeping promises that killed him by degrees.

But what if fear is the chain?

What if the thing they're running from is the only thing that could save them?

I wrote until my hand cramped, filling pages with dialogue, with revelation, with the slow unraveling of two fictional people who sounded too much like Wyatt and me to be coincidence.

The light had changed when I finally looked up. Late afternoon painted gold across the cave entrance. How long had I been here? My phone—

No signal. Of course.

I packed up the notebook, worked my way back out through the waterfall's spray. The forest had taken on that slanted light quality that meant sunset approached. I needed to move.

The trail—when I found it again after twenty minutes of controlled not-panic—was familiar as a friend. I half-jogged back, boots steady on the known terrain.

The cabin appeared through the trees just as the sun touched the western peaks. I fumbled for my phone as I crossed the threshold.

Three missed calls from Lily. Five texts.

Emma, are you okay?

Wyatt said your car's at the cabin but you're not answering.

Please just let me know you're alright.

I'm trying not to worry but it's been hours.

If you don't respond in the next hour I'm calling Search and Rescue.

Time stamp on the last one: eighteen minutes ago.

My fingers shook as I typed: *I'm fine. Sorry. Got turned around on the trail. No signal.*

Three dots appeared immediately. Then disappeared. Then appeared again.

Thank god. I was about to—

The message cut off. Started again.

Glad you're safe.

That was it. No questions about why I hadn't told anyone where I was going. No demands to know which trail, how I'd gotten lost. Just relief that I was okay.

I stared at the screen until it went dark.

In my notebook, Helena had finally told Jake the truth—that she loved him enough to stay if he loved her enough to choose. Not to promise, not to guarantee, just to choose. Every day. Even when it was hard. Even when leaving would be easier.

I opened my laptop, transferred the cave writings into pixels and bytes. The words flowed now, the dam broken. Chapter Twenty became Twenty-One, became Twenty-Two. Helena and Jake fought and made up and fought again, but differently now. Fighting toward each other instead of away.

Fifty thousand words became fifty-five, then sixty.

My phone buzzed. Email notification.

Jane Pierce, Literary Agent.

Subject: Checking In

Emma,

Just wanted to touch base on the manuscript progress. The publisher is very interested but needs to see the complete work by December 31st to include it in their spring catalog. How's the ending coming? Please tell me Helena and Jake figure it out. The world needs more happy endings, even if they're fictional.

-Jane

I started to type the truth—that I was stuck. Instead:

Making excellent progress. You'll have the full manuscript on schedule.

Send.

The lie sat in my stomach like a stone.

Outside, full darkness had arrived. Through the window, stars scattered across the sky like spilled salt. No light pollution here, just the vast sweep of the Milky Way and the shadow bulk of mountains beneath.

I shut the laptop, changed into sleep clothes—an old t-shirt and shorts that had seen better days. The bed welcomed me, soft and familiar after three months. The cabin had shaped itself around my routines, my rhythms. The coffee maker knew exactly how I liked my morning brew. The desk chair had molded to my posture. Even the shower had figured out that I preferred scalding hot water that would horrify anyone with sense.

Papers littered the floor around my desk—discarded scenes, false starts, descriptions that had felt important at three in the morning but rang hollow by dawn. I'd taken to printing pages just to crumple them, as if the physical act of destruction might clear space for something true.

One page lay near my foot, smoothed out after I'd balled it up, then retrieved it, then tried to throw it away again. The paragraph was visible even from here:

Helena's dream home wasn't grand. Just a place with honey-colored wood and light—the kind of light that made ordinary moments feel sacred. A kitchen where coffee tasted better. Windows that framed the mountains like art. Space enough for two people to exist without disappearing.

I'd written it at 2 AM, half-asleep, channeling Helena's deepest wish. The same wish I'd felt the first morning I woke up in this cabin, when the sun hit the pine walls just right and I'd thought: this. This is what home should feel like.

The page mocked me now. I picked it up, read it again, felt my throat tighten.

Honey-colored wood and light.

That's all I'd wanted. That's all Helena wanted. Not promises or grand gestures—just a place that felt like staying.

I crumpled it again, harder this time, and threw it toward the wastebasket. It bounced off the rim, rolled under the desk.

Good. Let it stay there with all the other discarded dreams.

This place felt like home.

The thought sent panic racing through my veins.

Not home. Temporary. A writing retreat that would end in December when I'd return to Seattle and my real life, away from Wyatt and Copper Ridge.

My phone glowed on the nightstand. No new messages from Wyatt. He was respecting the boundary I'd drawn, giving me the space I'd demanded.

So why did it feel like drowning?

I pulled the covers over my head, blocking out the stars and the phone and the manuscript that needed an ending I couldn't write. In the darkness, I could admit the truth—I knew exactly how Helena and Jake's story ended.

They chose each other. Despite the fear, despite the distance, despite everything that said it couldn't work.

But that was fiction.

In real life, firefighters left. Writers went back to Seattle. And flings stayed buried in the past where they belonged.

Didn't they?

The Price of a Home

♥

Emma

The phone rang while I stood at the kitchen sink, watching October rain streak the window. Dorothy's name on the screen made my stomach drop. She never called. In five months of renting, we'd exchanged only three texts about the wifi password.

"Emma, dear." Her voice was a dry rustle, the sound of something about to tear. "I need to tell you something."

I set down my coffee mug. The ceramic clicked against the granite counter, too loud in the morning quiet. "Is everything okay?"

"There's been an offer on the cabin."

The words hung between us. I gripped the edge of the sink, knuckles going white.

"An offer."

"From a developer. Mountain Vistas Properties." A rustling of papers came through the phone. "They want to tear it down. Build luxury vacation rentals. Offered me $500,000."

My reflection stared back from the dark window, a stranger. Who was that woman with the wide, haunted eyes? The mouth gone slack with shock? The mountains behind her were solid, permanent. She looked like a ghost already. Behind me, the cabin's familiar pine walls and stone fireplace looked exactly as they had five minutes ago. Before everything changed.

"When?" The word came out rough.

"They want possession by January first." Dorothy's breath hitched. "Emma, I'm so sorry. If there was any other way—"

"Your medical bills." I remembered her mentioning treatments, specialists in Denver.

"The insurance won't cover the new therapy. And this offer..." Another paper rustle. "It's enough to pay for everything. Maybe buy me a few more years."

A few more years. How could I begrudge her that?

"I understand."

"You can stay through December. I insisted on that. Give you time to—"

"Find somewhere else."

"Yes." Her voice dropped. "I know how much you love it there. How at home you've been. I wish—"

"It's okay, Dorothy." I pressed my free hand against my sternum, trying to ease the ache spreading through my chest. "Really. You need to do what's best for you."

We said goodbye with the awkward politeness of people trying not to hurt each other more. I set the phone down carefully, as if sudden movements might shatter something beyond repair.

I walked to the window seat, the one that looked out over the valley. In three weeks, the aspens had gone from scattered gold coins to full autumn fire. Soon they'd be bare. Then snow would come. Then January. Then—

Nothing.

My laptop beckoned from the desk. If I couldn't have this place, I needed to find another. Somewhere. Anywhere. Seattle again? Or here if...

Stop.

Seattle apartment listings blurred into a collage of gray walls and granite countertops. One listing in Belltown boasted "floor-to-ceiling windows" that looked out onto a concrete wall and the windows of a hundred strangers. It was smaller than the cabin's living room, surrounded by concrete and the constant hum of traffic. No mountains. No creek singing outside the window. No silence deep enough to hear your own heartbeat. The photo showed a smiling woman with a fake plant. Was that me now? A woman who settled for a sliver of sky between high-rises, pretending a plastic ficus was a forest?

The weather alert interrupted my scrolling. *Unusual early winter storm system developing. Potential for significant snow accumulation late October through early November. Residents advised to prepare.*

I glanced at the generator shed. Should check that. Make sure it worked before—

Another listing popped up. Queen Anne, mountain views. I clicked it. The "mountain view" was a sliver of Rainier between two high-rises if you stood in the right spot and squinted.

An hour passed. Two. The listings blurred together. Granite countertops, stainless steel appliances, "walkable neighborhood," "vibrant community," "urban lifestyle." Every description sounded like marketing copy because that's what it was. No one wrote the truth: "Box in the sky where you'll never know your neighbors' names."

My phone buzzed. Lily.

Coffee run to town?

I checked the time. Already noon. The morning had evaporated into apartment-hunting despair.

Sure. General store in 20?

I changed out of the flannel shirt and pulled on jeans and a sweater. My reflection looked presentable enough. Normal enough. Like someone whose life wasn't crumbling.

Twelve minutes to town. My hands knew the curves of the road. I passed the Sullivan Ranch, the scent of hay and horses thick in the air. The road dipped into an aspen grove—a suffocating tunnel of gold. Around the last bend, the fire station's red brick flashed between the trees. A punch to the gut. *His* station.

Wyatt's truck sat in the general store lot.

My hands tightened on the steering wheel. I could leave. Text Lily an excuse. But my gas gauge hovered near empty, and Patterson's had the only pumps in town.

I pulled into a gas pump, as far away from Wyatt's truck as I could. The autumn air bit sharp when I stepped out, carrying the scent of woodsmoke and dying leaves. Gray clouds massed overhead, promising the storm the weather service warned about.

The gas pump's numbers climbed slowly. $10, $15, $20. Movement in my peripheral vision made me glance up.

Wyatt emerged from the store, carrying a bag of what looked like replacement parts. He spotted me immediately. No escape now. He walked over with that easy stride that covered ground without seeming to hurry.

"Emma." He stopped a careful six feet away, respecting the boundary I'd drawn but hated. Dark circles shadowed his eyes. His hair needed a cut, curling over his collar in ways that made my fingers itch.

"Wyatt."

"How's the cabin?"

The question was casual. Small talk. The kind of thing you asked when you ran into someone you were trying not to care about. It knocked the air from my lungs.

"Being sold." The words came out flat. "Developer buying it. I have to be out by end of December."

His whole body went rigid. The bag in his hand crinkled as his grip tightened. "What?"

"Dorothy needs the money. Medical bills."

"But—" He stepped closer, then caught himself. "Where will you go?"

"Back to Seattle." I yanked the gas nozzle free, shoved it back in its cradle. "Where I should have stayed in the first place. I'll find another job."

Something shifted in his expression. The careful distance he'd been maintaining cracked. "You could stay."

"Stay where? The cabin's being demolished."

"Here. In Copper Ridge."

My laugh came out sharp enough to cut. "And do what? There's no work for a marketing consultant here. No apartment buildings. No—"

"There's me."

The words hung between us like a lit match over gasoline.

"What are you offering, Wyatt?" My voice rose, cracking on his name. "Another three days? A few weeks until the next fire calls you away?"

"I'm asking for a real chance." He moved closer, close enough that I could smell his soap, see the gold flecks in his gray eyes. "To finish what we started in Portland."

"We finished it. Five years ago. When I left and you let me."

"You disappeared. I got the message."

"And you accepted it." The gas pump receipt printed with a mechanical whir. I grabbed it, crumpled it in my fist. "You moved on. State to state, fire to fire, woman to woman—"

"There haven't been any other women." The admission came out rough. "Not... not the way you mean."

"Please." I fumbled for my keys. "Lily told me about the paramedic in Montana. The teacher in Oregon—"

"Dates. A few dinners. Nothing that—" He dragged a hand through his hair. "None of them were you."

"I'm not me either." The keys bit into my palm. "That woman in Portland who spent three days believing in fairy tales? She doesn't exist."

"Emma—"

"What would I be staying for?" The question ripped from my throat. "Tell me. What exactly would I be staying for?"

His mouth opened. Closed. The silence stretched until it snapped.

"That's what I thought." I wrenched the car door open.

"Portland was magical, and I know there's something between us that set us on fire. I'm not sure why you won't give me another chance." His voice broke on the words. "I know I'm bad at this. Emma, please."

"Trying isn't enough." I slid behind the wheel, couldn't look at him. "It never is."

I stomped on the gas, the tires spitting gravel. My own reflection in the rearview mirror was a cruel, tight-lipped woman I didn't recognize. I didn't look back. I couldn't. The ache in my chest was a vicious, satisfying burn. A shared wound.

The cabin welcomed me back with its familiar silence. I kicked off my shoes, ignored the blinking laptop, and curled into the window seat. The valley spread below, autumn painting the mountains in rust and gold. In two months, some developer would stand here calculating square footage and profit margins.

Outside, the first drops of rain hit the window. Not the usual autumn shower but something heavier, more insistent. The clouds had darkened to the color of old bruises. The weather service had mentioned snow possible at higher elevations.

I should check the generator.

Instead, I typed:

What does HEA look like when you don't believe in it?

The cursor blinked after the question mark. Seven words that summed up everything. How did you write a happy ending when you'd never seen one that lasted? When every promise turned into disappointment? When even the homes you found got torn down for profit?

The rain intensified, drumming against the roof. Somewhere out there, Wyatt was preparing for the storm. Checking equipment, making sure his crew was ready. Doing what he did best—showing up for emergencies but not for the everyday after.

I deleted the question and started again:

Helena stared at the empty apartment, boxes stacked against walls that would never feel like home.

Yes. That was it. The ending everyone feared but no one wanted to write. The realistic one. The one where the firefighter chose the fire and the woman chose herself and nobody got their heart broken because they'd been smart enough to protect it.

My phone buzzed. Wyatt.

I would stay for you.

I stared at the words until they blurred, tears running down my face because I couldn't hold them in any longer. Then I deleted his message, just like all the others.

Outside, the rain had turned to sleet, clicking against the windows like fingernails tapping for attention. The generator sat silent in its shed, unchecked, waiting for a storm that was already beginning.

Historic Snowfall

♥

Emma

The phone shrieked. I flinched, coffee sloshing over the rim of my mug as I grabbed it from the counter.

WINTER STORM WARNING: Historic early-season snowfall expected. 2-3 feet accumulation possible. Blizzard conditions likely. Prepare now.

I scrolled through the details. The system would arrive tomorrow afternoon, intensifying through the night. Mountain areas could see higher accumulations. Power outages likely. Travel will become impossible.

My gaze drifted to the window where the morning sun painted the peaks gold. Not a cloud in sight. Another 'historic' storm. I snorted, remembering the 'snowpocalypse' last month that had barely dusted the railings. The weather service needed to invest in a thesaurus.

Still, I wandered to the pantry. Three cans of soup, half a box of pasta, some stale crackers. The refrigerator held leftovers from two days ago, milk that would expire tomorrow, and a bottle of wine. Not exactly survival rations.

The firewood stack looked like a week's worth. I counted. It was maybe two days. My stomach tightened. The shed outside held more, but getting to it in a real storm...

I pulled on boots and headed to the generator shed. The red metal housing hadn't been opened in weeks. Spider webs stretched across the door handle. Inside, the generator squatted like a mechanical toad, covered in dust and pine needles.

The pull cord felt stiff in my hand. I yanked. Nothing. Again. The engine coughed, sputtered, died. On the third try, it caught with a reluctant rumble that smoothed into something almost steady. Almost.

A grinding noise scraped against my ears. Metal on metal, rhythmic and wrong. But it was running. That counted for something.

I should call someone. Mason would send Javi or one of the other firefighters to check it properly. Wyatt could—

No.

The generator hiccupped, steadied, continued its unhealthy rattle. It would be fine. Everything would be fine. I'd weathered Seattle winters. How much worse could a Colorado storm be?

Back inside, I made a list. Groceries, batteries, candles, more firewood from the shed. Simple preparations. I could handle this.

The drive to town felt different. The mountains seemed to lean in, watching. At Patterson's General Store, everyone moved with purpose. Ed Patterson stood behind the register, ringing up cases of water and bags of rock salt.

"Storm's gonna be a big one." He didn't look up from the register. "You prepared out there at the Ponderosa?"

"Getting there." I grabbed a basket, started filling it. Canned goods, batteries, matches.

"Generator working? Those old cabins, the power goes first."

"It's working," I said, the memory of that metallic grinding making my teeth ache. I needed to get out of here before he asked more questions.

"Wyatt was just in. Said they're putting everyone on standby. Haven't seen a November storm like this in twenty years."

My hands fumbled with a can of beans. It clattered to the floor. I bent to retrieve it, face burning. Of course Wyatt had been here. Of course Ed had to mention it.

I shoved my money at Ed, grabbing the receipt without waiting for the change, and loaded my car with the meager supplies. The radio crackled to life as I started the engine.

"...National Weather Service has upgraded the winter storm warning. Residents in mountain areas should complete all preparations immediately. This system has the potential to be life-threatening..."

I switched it off.

The cabin welcomed me back with its familiar quiet. I unpacked groceries, stacked them neatly in the pantry. See? Prepared. Ready. I didn't need anyone.

I settled into writing, losing myself in Helena's goodbyes. Outside, the sky began its shift from blue to gray.

The first snowflakes appeared just after noon. Fat, lazy things that drifted past the window like ash from some distant fire. Beautiful, really. I made tea, returned to the desk, kept writing.

By three o'clock, the lazy drift had become a steady fall. The mountains vanished first, erased behind a thick scrim of snow. Then the tree line. Then the edge of the meadow.

Wind rattled the windows. I added another log to the fire, pulled on a second sweater. The lights flickered. Once. Twice.

At five-thirty, darkness swallowed the cabin. The snow was horizontal now, driven by wind that howled around the corners of the cabin. I heated soup on the stove, ate standing at the counter, watching the storm intensify through the kitchen window.

The lights went out.

The world vanished. One second, the kitchen was lit; the next, I was in a void so complete I couldn't see the spoon in my own hand. The refrigerator hummed its last breath, the heater sighed into silence. Nothing left but the sound of the wind scraping at the walls, trying to get in.

The darkness wasn't just dark. It was the apartment in Portland after Mom left, when the power company shut everything off and Dad passed out on the couch. Ten years old, sitting in the corner of my room, listening to him snore while I shivered under a thin blanket. Waiting. Always waiting for someone to come, someone to fix it, someone to care enough to notice.

Not this time. I wasn't that girl anymore. I wasn't waiting for rescue.

Emergency lights. I felt my way to the flashlight drawer, clicked one on. The beam cut through darkness, revealing familiar furniture turned strange by shadows.

The generator. Right. This was why people had generators.

I pulled on my coat, grabbed the flashlight, pushed open the door. The wind nearly ripped it from my hands. Snow stung my face, ice crystals sharp as glass. I couldn't see the shed twenty feet away.

Fighting through knee-deep snow that hadn't been there earlier, I reached the generator shed. My fingers were already numb as I fumbled with the pull cord.

Nothing.

I yanked again. The cord bit into my frozen palm. Nothing. Just dead weight. "Come on, you bastard." The wind ripped the words from my mouth. I threw my whole body into the next pull. And the next. My shoulder lit up with hot, tearing pain. My fingers were useless claws, slipping on the cord.

The panic wasn't just about the cold. It was the helplessness. The being alone with no way out. The exact thing I'd spent my entire adult life running from, and here it was, waiting for me in a cabin in the middle of nowhere.

It wasn't going to start. It was dead. And I was going to die with it.

Back inside, I slammed the door against the storm. My phone showed 10% battery. How had I forgotten to charge it? When did I become so careless?

I called Lily. Straight to voicemail. Her phone was probably dead too, or she was somewhere without service. Mason next. No answer. The Copper Ridge Fire Station. Busy signal.

7% battery.

I typed a text to Wyatt: *Power out. Generator dead. Getting cold.*

Delete.

Started again: *I need help.*

Delete.

My finger hovered over the screen. Three words. That's all it would take. But I could see it so clearly—Wyatt arriving, taking over, fixing everything while I stood there useless and shaking. The damsel. The woman who couldn't handle her own life. The one who needed a man to save her.

Mom's voice echoed in my head, slurred and bitter: "Men leave, Emma. They always leave. And you know what's worse than being alone? Being the woman who waits for them to come back."

I wouldn't be her. I wouldn't be that.

Storm worse than expected. Cabin—

The phone died mid-word.

I set it down with careful precision, as if gentleness might resurrect it. The temperature was dropping fast without the heater. My breath misted in the flashlight beam.

Okay. Okay. People had survived centuries without electricity. I had a fireplace. Wood. Matches. This was manageable.

I dragged blankets and pillows to the hearth, built the fire up until it roared. The circle of warmth extended maybe six feet. Beyond that, the cabin grew colder by the minute.

Hours crawled past. I burned through the indoor wood supply, started breaking apart the dining chairs. Four chairs became fuel. Then the coffee table. The bookshelf.

By midnight—or what I thought was midnight—I was wearing every piece of clothing I owned. Two pairs of jeans. Three sweaters. My coat. Two pairs of socks inside my boots. A hat and hood pulled up. Wrapped in four blankets.

Still shivering.

The fire consumed furniture with horrifying speed. At this rate, I'd be burning the kitchen cabinets by dawn. If I made it to dawn.

My laptop sat on the mantel, manuscript trapped inside. Helena never got her ending. Neither did Jake.

"Should have given them the happy ending." My voice cracked. "Should have let them try."

The cold was a living thing now, pressing in from all sides. It crawled under the blankets, slipped through the layers of clothing, settled into my bones. My fingers were past numb, past hurting, into a strange tingling that probably meant damage.

My thoughts scattered, fragmented. The cold wasn't just physical anymore. It was every moment I'd ever been alone. Every time I'd chosen isolation over risk. Every door I'd closed before someone could close it on me.

This was what safety looked like. This was what independence got you. A woman freezing to death in a cabin, too proud to ask for help until it was too late.

I thought about Wyatt. His text that I'd deleted. *I would stay for you.*

Would he? Or was that just something you said when someone was leaving anyway? Easy to make promises you'd never have to keep.

The fire was dying. I'd fed it the last of the broken furniture, and now it consumed itself, logs collapsing into embers. I couldn't feel my toes. My thoughts moved through thick honey, slow and disconnected. The cold wasn't a monster anymore. It was a blanket. Heavy. Sinking into my bones, quieting the shivering. It wasn't a fight. It was a slow surrender. The thought of closing my eyes felt like the most wonderful thing in the world.

"Stupid." The word puffed white in the air. "So stupid."

I should have checked the generator properly. Should have called for help. Should have swallowed my pride and admitted I was in over my head. Should have, should have, should have.

My eyes drifted closed. So tired. The cold wasn't so bad when you stopped fighting it.

A sound cut through the wind's howl. Mechanical. Rhythmic.

My eyes snapped open. Was I hallucinating? The sound grew louder. An engine. A snowmobile engine.

I stumbled to the window, blankets falling away. A light pierced the white void. Real. Actual. Coming closer.

My frozen fingers fumbled with the door lock. The wind grabbed the door, slamming it against the wall. Snow erupted into the cabin, swirling, stinging.

A figure materialized from the storm. Tall, broad, covered head to toe in winter gear. The snowmobile's headlight backlit him, turning him into a dark, hulking shape against the white, then cut off.

He pushed through the door, slammed it shut, yanked off his helmet.

Wyatt.

Ice crystals clung to his stubble. His gray eyes swept the cabin—the dying fire, the broken furniture, me in my ridiculous layers—and his expression shifted from assessment to fury to terror in the span of a heartbeat.

"Are you insane?" The words exploded from him. "Do you have any idea how dangerous—" He stopped, took a breath that shook. "You could have died. You almost—Jesus, Emma."

I opened my mouth to respond. Nothing came out but a shudder that started in my chest and rippled outward until my whole body shook.

Rescue and Fury

Wyatt

The cold hit me first—not the storm's cold, but the bone-deep freeze radiating from Emma. Her lips had gone pale blue. Ice crystals clung to her lashes. She stood there in what looked like every piece of clothing she owned, trembling so hard her teeth chattered.

"Get by the fire." I dropped my helmet, grabbed her shoulders. Her body felt rigid under all those layers. "Now."

She stumbled toward the dying flames. I took in the cabin—broken chair legs scattered around the hearth, the coffee table in pieces, empty spaces where furniture should be. Christ. She'd been burning everything. A flash of white-hot rage surged through me. Her stubborn pride. Her goddamn stubborn pride had brought her to this—burning furniture to stay alive, too proud to call for help before her phone died, too proud to admit she needed anyone.

Then the rage collapsed into something worse. Terror. Pure, gut-wrenching terror that turned my knees to water. The broken furniture meant she'd been desperate. How long had she been out here alone, freezing, burning her belongings piece by piece? How close had I come to kicking down that door and finding her already gone? The thought hit like a fist to the chest. I've faced fire—walked into infernos that melted steel, pulled bodies from buildings seconds from collapse—but this feeling, this fear of losing her, was a thousand times worse.

"Blankets." My voice came out rough. "All of them."

Emma pointed to a pile near the fireplace with fingers that were clearly frozen. I wrapped two around her shoulders, forced her to sit close to what remained of the fire.

"I was f-fine until the p-power—"

"Fine?" The word exploded from me. I crouched in front of her, peeling off my gloves to check her hands. Ice cold. "You're eight miles from town. No power, no heat, no phone. In a blizzard that's dumping three feet of snow. How is that fine?"

Her eyes flashed despite the exhaustion. "I didn't ask you to—"

"To what? Save your life?" I stood, paced to the window. Nothing but white void. The wind screamed against the glass. "Lily called Mason in tears because you weren't answering. The whole station's been trying to reach you for hours."

"My phone died."

"Of course it did." I pulled out my radio, the weight of it familiar in my hand. "And the generator?"

"It was working earlier. Sort of."

"Sort of." I shook my head. "I need to check it."

I grabbed the flashlight from my pack, headed back into the storm. The generator shed stood twenty feet away and snow had drifted against the door. I yanked it open.

One look was all it took. The starter was scorched black, the whole damn motor seized tight. It was a metal corpse. Useless.

Back inside, I stomped snow from my boots. Emma hadn't moved from her spot by the fire.

"Generator's dead. Completely shot."

She pulled the blankets tighter.

I switched on my radio. Static filled the cabin, then Mason's voice cut through.

"Wyatt, you there?"

"Yeah. Made it to the Ponderosa."

"Emma?"

"Alive. Half-frozen, but alive." I watched her flinch at the words. "Generator's fried. We're on fireplace only."

A long pause. Mason knew what that meant.

"Roads are gone, brother. Highway patrol just closed everything. This storm's not moving—weather service says five days minimum. Maybe longer."

The air seemed to compress. Emma's head snapped up.

"Say again?"

"Five days. You're stuck. Both of you."

Emma's eyes widened. "Five days?"

"Copy that." I clicked off before Mason could say more.

The only sound was the wind, a physical presence trying to tear the cabin apart. It was a silence that felt heavier than the storm, filled with everything we'd spent years not saying. Five days. Trapped in this cabin with the woman who'd been haunting me for five years. The woman who'd spent three months avoiding me like I carried plague.

"You should go." Emma's voice barely carried over the storm. "Before it gets worse."

"Go?" I stared at her. "Go where? You heard Mason. Roads are closed."

"But you got here—"

"On a snowmobile in conditions that nearly killed me twice. Visibility's zero. Temperature's dropping. I try to leave now, they'll find my frozen corpse in a snowbank come spring."

She looked away. "There has to be another option."

"There isn't." I headed back outside to grab my emergency pack from the snowmobile. The wind tried to rip the bag from my hands. By the time I made it back inside, fresh snow coated everything.

I dropped the pack by the door, started pulling out supplies. Emergency sleeping bag rated to minus twenty. MREs—enough for three days if we rationed. First aid kit. Water purification tablets. Backup flashlight. Batteries.

"You can't stay here."

I stopped unpacking. "Trust me, I'd rather not."

The hurt that flashed across her face made something twist in my chest.

"That's not—" I ran a hand through my hair, spraying water droplets. "Emma, this isn't about us. This is about not dying."

"I know that."

"Do you? Because you nearly froze to death tonight."

"I was managing."

"Managing?" I gestured at the destroyed furniture. "You burned your dining set."

"It was that or freeze."

"You could have called for help."

"My phone—"

"Before it died. When the storm started. When the generator first had problems." Each word came out harder than the last. "But you didn't, because you'd rather die than admit you need anyone."

She stood, blankets falling away. Even through the layers of clothing, I could see her shaking. "You don't get to lecture me about needing people. You're the one who runs. Always. It's what you do."

"I'm here now."

"Because Mason made you come."

"No." The word came out quiet. "Mason told me you were in trouble. Nobody made me gear up in a blizzard and drive eight miles through zero visibility. I did that because I was worried about you."

She blinked, swayed slightly.

I caught her arms, steadied her. "When was the last time you ate?"

"I... this morning. Maybe."

"Sit." I guided her back to the floor. "I'll heat something up."

The kitchen was arctic. I lit the stove with matches from my pack, grateful she had propane. Found a pot, dumped in two cans of soup from her meager supplies. While it heated, I hauled in more wood from the covered stack outside the door. Not much—maybe two days' worth if we were careful.

"Here." I handed her the mug of soup. "Drink it slow."

She wrapped her hands around the ceramic. "How did you know? That I was in trouble?"

"Lily called the station, frantic. Then Mason's voice on the radio, tight with a worry he was trying to hide. The power grids started failing, and all we got from your number was silence." I shook my head, the memory of the drive—blind faith and sheer terror—still raw. "Someone had to come."

"And that someone was you."

"I know these mountains. Know the landmarks even in whiteout conditions. And I had the gear."

"Your job."

"Yeah. My job."

She took another sip of soup. Color was returning to her cheeks. "What about the fire crew? Don't they need you?"

"They've got backup from Ridgeway. Mason can handle things."

"For five days?"

"For however long it takes."

The weight of those words settled between us. Five days minimum. Maybe longer. No escape, no buffer, no avoiding each other. Just us and the storm and whatever had been simmering between us since Portland.

I checked my watch. Midnight. "We need to set up a rotation for the fire. Can't let it die completely."

"I can—"

"We'll take shifts. Two hours each. That way nobody gets too exhausted."

She nodded, not arguing for once.

I spread my sleeping bag on one side of the hearth, gestured for her to take the other. She'd already dragged blankets and pillows there. The living room furniture had been reduced to kindling, but at least we had a clear space around the fireplace.

"What about food?"

"I've got enough MREs for three days. You've got some cans. We ration carefully, we'll make it."

"Water?"

"We can melt snow. I brought purification tablets just in case."

She stared into the flames. "You really thought of everything."

"It's what I do. Prepare for worst-case scenarios."

"Is that what this is? Worst case?"

Worst case? I bit back the words. *Worst case was the image burned behind my eyes—kicking in that door, the flashlight beam cutting through the freezing dark, half-expecting to find your body.* The thought still made my stomach clench. The wave of relief that hit when I saw you standing, breathing, had been so strong it buckled my knees. "No," I said, my voice steady despite the memory. "I've been in worse."

"When you're jumping into wildfires."

"Yeah."

She made a sound that might have been a laugh. "The storm or each other. Which do you think will kill us first?"

"Emma—"

"I'm going to bed." She burrowed into her pile of blankets, turned her back to me.

I fed another log to the fire, watched the flames catch and grow. Outside, the storm raged, shaking the cabin like it wanted in. The temperature had to be near zero already. Would drop to minus ten by morning. Without the fire, we'd be ice sculptures by dawn.

Five days.

I'd survived explosions. Building collapses. Forty-foot falls. Sixth-degree burns that nearly killed Mac three years back. But five days trapped with Emma? That might actually finish me.

She shifted in her blankets, and I caught a glimpse of her face in the firelight. The shadows under her eyes, the worry line between her brows that appeared whenever she concentrated on something. She'd lost weight since the wedding. Since that dance when she'd felt perfect in my arms before remembering all the reasons we couldn't work.

My radio crackled. "Wyatt, you copy?"

Mason again. I grabbed it before the noise could wake her, though her breathing told me she wasn't really asleep.

"Copy."

"You two okay?"

I looked at Emma, curled in her blankets, pretending to sleep. At the broken furniture. The meager supplies. The way she'd almost died tonight rather than ask for help.

"We're stuck. For however long this takes. We're going to have to figure out how to survive this."

Mason's pause said he understood. "Good luck, brother."

The radio went silent. I set it aside, settled against the wall where I could watch the fire and the door. First watch was mine. In two hours, I'd wake Emma for her turn. Then we'd switch again. And again. For five days. Maybe longer. I could think of a dozen ways to keep warm and most of them involved Emma.

The wind screamed louder, like it was angry at being locked out. Snow piled against the windows, blocking out even the faint hope of starlight. We were alone. Cut off. No rescue coming.

Just us. The storm. And the ghost of Portland that had haunted me for years.

Bunkhouse Habits

♥

Emma

The manuscript pages lay scattered across the cabin floor. I dropped to my knees, gathering them with numb fingers while Wyatt hauled his gear to the far side of the fireplace. Chapter 8 under the coffee table. Chapter 15 near the door. Two years of work thrown around by my frantic search for something—anything—to burn.

"Here." Wyatt held out a page that had drifted near his pack.

I snatched it from his hand. The confrontation scene where everything fell apart.

His eyes tracked the title at the top of the page. "Smoke and Surrender?"

Heat crawled up my neck. I shuffled the page into my stack, not meeting his gaze.

"You're writing a romance novel?"

"A novel." I stood, hugging the pages to my chest. "It happens to have romance in it."

He unrolled his sleeping bag with precise movements, each corner squared perfectly. "About firefighters?"

"Wildland firefighters." The distinction mattered, though I couldn't explain why.

His hands stilled on the sleeping bag's zipper. A log popped in the hearth. Outside, the wind hammered the glass, demanding a way in.

"Let me guess." His voice dropped, rough at the edges. "He leaves. She stays. Tragic ending."

My grip tightened on the manuscript. "I haven't decided on the ending yet."

"Well." He smoothed a wrinkle from the sleeping bag with unnecessary focus. "I hope he's smarter than I was."

A silence settled, heavier than the snow piling against the door. I turned away, stacking the pages on the kitchen counter where they'd be safe from stray sparks. My hands shook. From cold, I told myself. Just cold.

It was my turn for watch, to keep the fire going and make sure everything was ok. I fed another piece of what used to be a dining chair to the fire. The wood caught fast, painted surface bubbling before flame consumed it. Two hours. I could handle two hours.

Wyatt shifted in his sleeping bag, and I found myself tracking the sound. The rustle of nylon. His breathing evening out. How many nights had I spent wondering where he was sleeping? Alaska. California. Montana.

"Stop staring at me."

I jerked my gaze back to the fire. "I wasn't—"

"You were." He sat up, sleeping bag pooling at his waist. "Might as well talk if we're both awake."

"You should rest. Long day tomorrow."

"Every day's long when you're snowed in." He leaned back against the wall, watching me across the orange glow. "You made it pretty clear at the party that you think I'm a coward."

The accusation hit like cold water. "What?"

"The engagement party. Your exact words were 'at least I'm not the only coward here.'"

Months ago, but the memory burned fresh. Standing in the parking lot, him demanding to know why I'd left Portland, why I'd never called. The hurt in his eyes when I'd thrown his leaving back at him like a weapon.

"You made it clear you think I'm a flight risk."

"Aren't you?" The question tasted bitter. "How many states this year? Oregon, California, Montana—"

"That's my job. I save lives."

"And I'm not asking you to change that."

A sharp, hollow sound escaped him. It wasn't a real laugh. "No, you just decided for me."

The accusation landed like a punch. He wasn't wrong. I could still picture that Portland hotel room, the gray morning light filtering through the blinds. I'd watched him sleep, his bag already packed by the door, and a cold certainty had settled in my bones. I could love this man with everything I had, and he would still leave. He would always leave.

I looked away from him, toward the fire. "People like you don't stay," I said, my voice a whisper. "It's not in your nature."

"You don't know my nature."

Silence stretched between us. The storm hammered at the walls, testing every board, every nail. I added another chair leg to the fire.

"My dad died when I was thirteen."

The words came from nowhere, soft enough I almost missed them.

I turned. Wyatt stared at the ceiling, jaw working.

"Wildfire. He was cutting line, trying to save the Jacobsen ranch." His voice stayed flat, matter-of-fact. "Wind shifted. They didn't even find his body for three days."

"Wyatt—"

"Mason was sixteen. James was ten. Someone had to take care of us, and Mason stepped up. Gave up his college scholarship. Gave up leaving. Gave up everything."

The fire popped. A log shifted, sending up a shower of sparks.

He stared into the flames, grabbing the poker and aggressively jabbing at a log. "I watched what staying did to Mason. He gave up everything. For us. And some days... some days I see the cost in his eyes." He dropped the poker with a clatter. "So, yeah. I keep moving. It's cleaner that way."

Something shifted in my chest. The certainty I'd carried for five years—that Wyatt left because leaving was easy for him—cracked down the middle. I thought of my mother, waiting. I thought of Mason, trapped. Two different prisons, both built from staying.

Wyatt wasn't running from me. He was running from becoming his brother.

The realization settled over me like snow, quiet and inevitable. All this time, I'd seen his leaving as proof he didn't care enough. But maybe it was proof he cared too much. About everyone he might hurt. Everyone who might need him to stay.

"Mason doesn't resent you," I said softly. "He chose to stay."

"Did he? Or did my dad's death choose for him?" Wyatt's voice was raw. "I won't do that to someone. Won't let them sacrifice everything because I can't handle being alone."

My throat tightened. Wasn't that what I'd been afraid of? That I'd sacrifice everything, and he'd leave anyway? But I'd been so focused on my own fear, I'd never considered his.

His face changed, something raw flashing across his features before he looked away.

"Your turn's up."

Two hours exactly. Of course he'd been tracking time even while talking.

We switched positions in awkward silence. Him feeding the fire, me crawling into blankets that smelled like woodsmoke. The floor felt harder than I'd expected, even with the couch cushions I'd salvaged.

"Emma."

I kept my eyes closed.

"I'm sorry. About your manuscript. About almost losing it."

"It's just paper."

"No, it's not."

He was right. It was two years of wrestling my feelings onto pages, trying to write my way to an understanding.

I must have dozed, because suddenly the windows showed grey instead of black. Dawn filtering through snow. The storm still raged, but morning had found us.

Coffee. I smelled coffee.

Wyatt stood at the stove, his back to me, working with the ancient percolator I'd found in the cupboard. Steam rose from the spout, carrying that perfect morning smell that made everything seem possible.

"How?"

"Emergency instant coffee in my pack. But you had this old thing, and I figured..." He shrugged, still not turning around. "Figured real coffee might help."

I pulled myself up, muscles protesting every movement. The fire still crackled, well-fed and steady. He'd kept it going all night.

"My dad was in the military."

The words surprised me as much as him. He turned, coffeepot in hand.

"Gone ten months out of every twelve. Sometimes more." I accepted the mug he offered, warmth seeping into my frozen fingers. "I spent my childhood watching my mother wait by a phone that never rang. I won't be her."

The coffee burned my tongue, but I drank it anyway. Needed something to do with my hands, my mouth, anything to avoid seeing understanding dawn in his eyes.

"That's why you left Portland."

My throat closed.

"You knew I'd leave too."

"Your whole life is leaving. It's who you are."

"Maybe." He sat down across from me, his own mug cradled in his hands. "Or maybe I just haven't found a reason to stay."

The weight of that hung between us. Four more days trapped here, trying to figure out if we were writing a tragedy or something else.

Outside, the wind screamed its fury, and snow continued to fall.

Splitting the Silence

♥

Wyatt

My breath clouded in the cabin air, each exhale a small ghost that dissipated before reaching the ceiling. Day three. The storm hadn't let up—if anything, the wind hit harder now, testing every joint and seal in the cabin's construction. Ice crystals formed on the inside of the window frames despite the fire I'd kept burning all night.

Emma sat at the kitchen table, wrapped in every blanket she owned, her notebook open in front of her. She'd been writing since dawn, pen scratching across paper in quick bursts followed by long pauses where she stared at nothing. Her fingers, poking out of fingerless gloves, had gone pink with cold.

"We need to seal those gaps." I stood, joints protesting after hours of sitting vigil by the fire. "The temperature's dropping faster than the fire can compensate."

She looked up, glasses slightly fogged. "What gaps?"

I walked to the nearest window, ran my hand along the frame. Cold air leaked through, steady as a river current. "Here. And probably around the door, under the baseboards. This place wasn't built for this kind of cold."

"Can we fix it?"

"We can try." I opened my pack, pulled out the duct tape I always carried. "But first, we need more wood. What we have won't last another day."

Emma set down her pen, determination replacing the distant look she got when writing. "I can help."

"You know how to split wood?"

"I can learn."

She stood, shedding blankets like armor, revealing the oversized flannel shirt she'd thrown over her thermal top. My flannel, I realized. She must have grabbed it from where I'd left it drying by the fire.

Outside, the cold hit like a physical blow. The woodpile sat twenty feet from the door, half-buried under fresh snow. I grabbed the axe from where it leaned against the cabin wall, ice crackling off the handle.

"Watch first." I positioned myself at the chopping block, selected a decent-sized log. The axe came up smooth, years of muscle memory guiding the arc. The blade bit deep, splitting the wood with a satisfying crack.

Emma stood close enough that I caught her shampoo scent despite the wind. Lavender. How she still smelled like lavender after three days in a snowstorm defied logic.

"Your turn." I handed her the axe.

The weight caught her off guard. She adjusted her grip, lifted it awkwardly overhead, and brought it down. The blade glanced off the log's edge, burying itself in the chopping block inches from her boot.

"Jesus, Emma—"

"I'm fine." She yanked the axe free, face flushed with more than cold. "Let me try again."

"Wait." I moved around behind her. "Your grip is wrong."

She tensed as I approached but didn't step away. I reached around, adjusted her hands on the handle. "Lower. Like this."

My chest pressed against her back. Her warmth cut through both our layers of clothing, and suddenly the frozen morning didn't feel quite so cold. My hands covered hers on the axe handle, guiding the position.

"Feel the weight of it." My voice came out rougher than intended. "Let gravity do most of the work."

She nodded, a tiny movement I felt more than saw. Her breathing had changed, quickened. We stood frozen, neither quite willing to acknowledge what was happening.

"Lift from here." I guided her arms up, the movement bringing us closer. "Then—"

The axe came down, guided by both our hands. The log split clean.

We stayed there a heartbeat too long, her back against my chest, our hands still gripping the axe handle. A slow burn started in my gut, spreading through my veins until the tips of my ears were hot.

Emma pulled away, "I've got it now." My hands felt empty. I took a step back, and the sub-zero air hit my chest where she'd just been. "Right," I said, "Yeah. You've got it."

She hefted the axe again, this time managing a respectable swing that actually split wood. We worked in silence after that, stealing glances when we thought the other wasn't looking. Every time our hands brushed passing logs, every accidental bump as we navigated the narrow path back to the cabin, and the air went sharp and thin, like it did right before a lightning strike.

Inside, we shed our snow-covered outer layers and got to work on the windows. The kitchen forced us into close quarters—shoulders brushing as we sealed gaps, hands tangling when we both reached for the tape. Emma's cheeks stayed flushed, and I told myself it was from the cold.

"Pass me that towel?" She gestured to the counter behind me.

I turned, grabbed it, turned back to find her closer than expected. Close enough to count the freckles across her nose. Close enough to see her pulse jumping at her throat.

"Thanks." She took the towel, fingers grazing mine.

We sealed three windows before the silence got too heavy. Emma opened a can of soup, set it on the stove. The kitchen barely had room for one person, let alone two, but I joined her, pulling crackers from my pack.

"Why smokejumping?" She stirred the soup with focused attention, like Campbell's chicken noodle required technique. "Of all the firefighting jobs, why the one that drops you into hell from a plane?"

I leaned against the counter, close enough that our hips almost touched. "Seemed like the job where I could make the biggest difference. Jump into impossible situations, save what could be saved, move on—"

"Before what?"

Before anyone could depend on me. Before I could disappoint them.

"Before things got complicated."

Emma turned to face me fully. In the tiny kitchen, that meant we stood inches apart. "And the moving on part never bothered you?"

"Never did before."

The word hung between us. Before. Before Portland. Before her. Before I knew what I was missing.

She searched my face, looking for something. Truth, maybe. Or lies. I didn't know which would hurt her less.

The soup bubbled over.

"Shit—" Emma spun back to the stove, grabbing the pot with her bare hand. She yelped, dropped it. Soup splattered across the floor.

"Let me see." I caught her wrist, examined the angry red mark across her palm.

"It's fine—"

"It's not." I guided her to the sink, turned on the tap. The water ran ice cold. She hissed as it hit the burn but didn't pull away. I kept her hand under the stream, my fingers gentle around her wrist.

"This is stupid." Her voice shook. "Can't even heat soup without—"

"Without what? Being human?"

She looked up at me then, eyes bright with frustration and something else. We stood there, her burned hand between us under the running water, and the air went thick.

I turned off the tap. Reached for a clean dish towel, wrapped her hand carefully. She watched me work, bottom lip caught between her teeth.

"Thank you."

"MREs for lunch?" I kept my voice light, stepping back before I did something stupid. "They're harder to spill."

That earned me a small laugh. We cleaned up the soup disaster together, heated MREs instead, and ate standing at the counter because sitting meant not being close enough to share warmth.

Evening fell early, the grey light fading to black by four o'clock. We gravitated to the fireplace, the only real heat source left as the temperature continued dropping. I fed logs to the flames while Emma settled on the floor with her notebook, back against the couch frame.

I sat beside her—not touching, but close enough that our shared body heat created a small pocket of warmth. She wrote in quick bursts, pen flying across paper, then long pauses where she tapped the pen against her lips.

I found myself reading over her shoulder. Not intentionally at first, but her handwriting drew me in. The scene she worked on involved two characters stuck in a fire tower during a storm. The parallel wasn't lost on me.

"'He watched her across the narrow space,'" I read aloud, "'wondering if the walls between them were made of wood or something less solid but harder to break.'"

Emma's pen stilled. "You're reading my work."

"You're letting me."

She turned her head slightly, not quite looking at me. "It's terrible."

"It's not."

Emma's breath caught. She turned to face me fully, and we sat there, shoulders pressed together, her notebook forgotten in her lap. The firelight caught the gold in her green eyes, turned her skin warm despite the cold pressing against the windows.

The notebook slipped from her lap. Neither of us moved to retrieve it. We sat there, shoulders touching, sharing warmth and something more. Something in my chest, a knot I'd been carrying for fourteen years, started to unravel. It left an ache behind, a hollow space that felt a hell of a lot like hope.

Emma's hand rested on the floor between us. I covered it with mine, careful of her burn. She didn't pull away.

Outside, the storm raged. Inside, the silence was just as loud. And something in me, something I thought was frozen solid, started to thaw.

The Pride and Prejudice of Portland

Wyatt

The last candle sputtered, wax pooling at its base. An hour of light, tops. Outside, the storm hammered the walls like it wanted in.

I dealt another hand of gin rummy, the cards worn soft from three days of handling. Emma sat cross-legged on the floor, her back against the couch, that oversized flannel of mine hanging off one shoulder. The bandage on her palm caught the firelight every time she rearranged her cards.

"You're cheating." She narrowed her eyes at my discard pile.

"You can't prove that."

"You've won six hands in a row."

"Skill." I kept my face a blank mask. She was right. I'd been counting since game two. An old bunkhouse habit—when you can't control the world outside, you control the cards in your hand.

She drew a card, studied her hand with the kind of focus she usually reserved for her notebook. The firelight turned her skin gold, made shadows dance across her collarbone where my shirt gaped open.

"Your brother really gave up Colorado State for you?" The question came casual, but her eyes stayed on her cards.

My fingers tightened on my hand. Seven of hearts, two jacks. Nothing worth keeping.

"Yeah."

"That must have been hard to watch."

The fire popped, sending sparks up the chimney. Outside, wind rattled the windows in their frames despite our duct tape patches.

"Dad died in October." The cards in my hand felt like flimsy paper. "Mason had just started his sophomore year. Full ride, engineering program. He was going to design bridges."

Emma's cards lowered to her lap.

"I was thirteen. James was ten. Child services showed up the day after the funeral, ready to split us up. Foster homes. Maybe adoption if we were lucky, but not together. Not three boys with baggage."

My throat felt thick. I grabbed the water bottle beside me, took a long drink.

"Mason drove from Colorado Springs that day. Walked into that meeting still wearing his college sweatshirt and told them he was taking custody. Twenty years old, and he signed his life away for us."

"That's not signing his life away. That's choosing family."

"Is it?" I slapped my cards on the table, the sound cracking in the quiet. "He worked construction during the day, took night classes at community college. Gave up his dreams so James and I could stay a family. Never complained, never made us feel guilty, but I saw it. The acceptance letters he threw away. The job offers he turned down because they meant moving us."

Emma shifted closer, her knee brushing mine. The contact sent heat through my jeans.

"You think staying means sacrificing everything you want."

It wasn't a question. It was the truth that had shaped my entire life. "Doesn't it?" I picked up my cards again, needing something to do with my hands. "Look at Mason. Seventeen years in the same town, same job, same—"

"Same job he loves. Same town that respects him. Same life he built just how he wanted it." Emma's voice carried a certainty that made me look up. "You think he sacrificed, but what if he just chose? What if Copper Ridge and the station and raising you—what if that became his dream?"

The cards bent in my grip. I set them down before I ruined the deck. "That's different."

"Why?"

"Because he had to. There was no choice."

"There's always a choice." Emma tucked a strand of hair behind her ear, the gesture so familiar it made my chest ache. "He could have let child services take you. Could have visited on weekends. Could have waited until you aged out. But he chose you. Every day for seventeen years, he chose you and James."

I stared at the fire, watching flames consume the log I'd added an hour ago. The wood cracked, split, fell into glowing coals.

"What about you?" I grabbed for a subject change before the conversation cut any deeper. "The writing. When did that start?"

Emma's shoulders relaxed, accepting the redirect. "College. Creative writing minor my mother hated. 'You can't eat dreams, Emma.' She wanted me in business, something practical."

"But you kept writing."

"In secret. Late nights after work. Weekends. Two years on this manuscript, and I still can't get the ending right." She picked up her cards again, shuffled them without looking. "My characters keep getting stuck in the same argument. Like they're afraid of being happy."

We played three more hands in comfortable silence, the fire crackling between us. I won two, she won one, though I suspected she'd started counting cards too.

"I fought fire in Oregon that summer." The log in the grate popped, spitting an ember onto the hearth. "After Portland."

Emma's hands stilled on her cards.

"Rookie season with the McKenzie crew. Fourteen-hour days in hundred-degree heat. Best job I ever had, besides the one that almost killed me twice." I laughed, short and hard. "Ended up with a rare weekend off. Contractual requirement. Couldn't work us twenty-one days straight, apparently."

"Drove into Portland because I couldn't stand another night in the bunkhouse. Found this dive bar near the university. Dark enough to disappear in, cheap enough for a rookie's salary."

Emma set down her cards completely, giving me her full attention.

"You were at a table near the window. Three other women, all of you arguing about something. Your hands moved when you talked, these big gestures that kept knocking over your beer. One of your friends kept having to catch it."

The world shifted. That's the only way to describe it. Like every axis I'd been spinning on suddenly tilted, and gravity pulled in a different direction. Toward her. I'd seen beautiful women before—plenty of them. But this was different. This was recognition, like my soul had been waiting for hers to walk into that bar.

"Jane." Emma's voice came out rough. "My college roommate. She was defending Wickham."

"And you were destroying her entire argument with citations from the text." I shook my head, the memory so clear I could smell the stale bar air. "You actually had a paperback copy of Pride and Prejudice in your purse. Started reading passages out loud to prove your point."

Emma's hand covered her mouth, but I caught the smile underneath.

"'How despicably I have acted,'" I quoted, the words coming back perfect after five years. "'I, who have prided myself on my discernme nt.'"

"You remember that?"

"I remember everything." The fire seemed to dim, sucking the air from the room. I couldn't look at her. If I did, she'd see it all. "The way you laughed when Jane threw a napkin at your head. How you tucked your hair behind your ear when you got flustered. The exact shade of green your dress was—like forest moss after rain."

A sharp hiss of air escaped Emma's lips.

"Your friends left around midnight. You stayed. Moved to the bar, ordered whiskey neat, which surprised the hell out of me after watching you nurse light beer all night."

"Liquid courage." She pulled her knees up to her chest, my flannel pooling around her. "I saw you watching. Figured if I didn't talk to you, I'd regret it forever."

"You asked if I had opinions about Darcy's character arc."

"And you said, 'Depends. Are we talking about the Darcy who proposes the first time, or the one who learns from his mistakes?'"

We sat there, five years collapsed into nothing, that Portland bar more real than the cabin around us.

"Three days." My voice dropped lower. "Three days that felt like three years. Like I'd known you my whole life."

Emma's eyes shimmered in the firelight. "We talked about everything. Books, movies, whether aliens existed, the best way to make coffee. You told me about fighting fires, made it sound like poetry instead of hell."

"You told me about wanting to write. Read me a story you'd scribbled on napkins at three in the morning."

"You said it was good."

"It was." I reached for the poker, stirred the coals just to have something to do with my hands. "That Sunday morning, you made coffee in my hotel room. Terrible hotel coffee that you somehow made taste perfect. We watched the sun rise over the river, and you said—"

"'I could do this forever.'" Emma's voice cracked. "I meant it."

"So why did you leave?"

The question hung in the air like smoke. Emma pulled the flannel tighter around herself, suddenly small.

"I had to get back. Work. Life. All the responsible things that seemed to matter before I met you."

Bullshit. Complete bullshit, and we both knew it. But she wasn't ready to give me more, and pushing would only make her shut down.

I let it go. For now.

The truth sat heavy in my chest, the confession I couldn't make out loud. I didn't look for you. After you left, after I got back to Copper Ridge, after the season ended and I had all the time in the world—I didn't look. I told myself it was because you'd made your choice, walking out of that hotel room without leaving a number, an email, anything. But that was a lie. The real reason was simpler, more pathetic. I was a coward. Afraid that if I found you, the reality wouldn't match the memory. That you'd be ordinary. That the connection I felt was just loneliness and good timing. Or worse—so much worse—that it would all be real. That you'd be everything I remembered and more. That I'd have to choose. Have to change everything. So I did nothing. Kept you perfect and untouchable in my head, a story I could control. And hated myself a little more each year for it.

We abandoned the card game, neither of us able to focus. Emma grabbed her notebook, settled closer to the fire with her back against the couch. Give her space. Bank the fire. Go outside and freeze your ass off. My brain listed the sensible options. I ignored all of them and watched her write.

The candlelight had died completely, leaving only the fire to light her work. She bent close to the page, squinting without her glasses. Her pen moved in quick bursts—a flurry of words, then nothing. She'd tap the pen against her lips, think, then attack the page again.

"What?"

She'd caught me staring. Hair falling from her bun, my shirt sliding off her shoulder, bandaged hand holding the notebook steady—she was a beautiful, chaotic mess that I'd been running from for five years. The thought formed, solid and undeniable, and was out of my mouth before I could stop it. "You're even more beautiful than I remembered."

The pen slipped from her fingers. We stared at each other across two feet of space that felt like miles and nothing all at once. The firelight caught the gold flecks in her eyes, turned her lips the color of wine.

I started to lean forward. She swayed toward me. The space contracted, disappeared—

"Please." Her voice a whisper. "Don't."

She grabbed her notebook and retreated to the kitchen, leaving me alone with the dying fire. The wind howled, mocking the silence inside. Nothing. She'd given me nothing, just like before. And I was left staring into the flames, asking the same damn question I'd been asking for five years.

The Ring in the Purse

♥

Emma

Warmth. That was the first thing that registered—a cocoon of heat that had nothing to do with the dying fire across the room. I floated in that half-awake space where the world hadn't solidified yet, where I could pretend the storm had been a dream and I was back in Seattle, safe in my apartment with its predictable walls and locked doors.

But Seattle apartments didn't smell like woodsmoke and pine. They didn't have this solid presence at my back, radiating heat through worn cotton. They didn't have an arm draped across my waist, holding me like I was something precious.

My eyes snapped open.

Gray morning light filtered through frost-etched windows. The fire had burned down to embers, just a faint glow in the grate. We were on the floor in front of the couch, a tangle of limbs and shared blankets.

Wyatt's chest rose and fell against my back in the steady rhythm of deep sleep. His arm anchored me against him, and I'd somehow threaded my fingers through his during the night.

This is how it starts.

The thought sliced through me like a blade.

This is how it starts. You get comfortable. You start to need them. And then they leave.

A sudden awareness shot through me. The rough weave of his thermal shirt against my cheek. The solid, slow beat of his heart under my ear. The scent of him—woodsmoke, pine, and something uniquely Wyatt that made my lungs ache. We fit together like we'd been sleeping this way for years instead of accidentally gravitating together in unconscious need.

You let yourself have this—the warmth, the safety, the feeling that someone actually wants you there. You start to believe it's real. You start to trust it.

And that's when they see who you really are. That's when they realize you're not worth staying for.

I needed to move. Now. Before he woke up and made this real.

Before I started to need this. Before I need him so much it hurts to leave.

My attempt to slide away made his arm tighten.

"Emma." His voice was a low rasp, thick with sleep. "Don't move yet."

My heart slammed against my ribs. "Wyatt, we can't—"

"I know." His words ghosted across my neck. "Just... five more seconds."

Five seconds to want something. Five seconds to let my guard down. Five seconds closer to the inevitable moment when he walks away.

I should have pulled away. Should have put the necessary distance between us before this got worse. Instead, I let myself sink back into him. Let myself have this—the weight of his arm, the solid wall of his chest, the way he held me like letting go would break something fundamental.

Five seconds became ten. Became thirty. Became a minute of just breathing together while the storm whispered against the windows and the world beyond this cabin ceased to exist.

His thumb moved against my stomach where his hand rested, just the smallest stroke through the flannel. That tiny movement shattered whatever spell had held us frozen.

This is how it starts. And I know exactly how it ends.

I jerked away, stumbling to my feet so fast the room tilted.

My throat felt tight, forcing the words out. "I need—bathroom."

Wyatt pushed himself into a sitting position, his movements stiff from the hard floor. His hair was sticking up at angles that would have been endearing if I could afford to find anything about him endearing. He didn't say anything, just watched me flee with those gray eyes that saw too much.

The bathroom mirror reflected a disaster. Hair tangled beyond salvation, eyes puffy from poor sleep, his flannel hanging on me like I was playing dress-up in someone else's life. I twisted the faucet and plunged my hands into the icy water, splashing it on my face again and again. The shock of it was a clean pain, a welcome sting against my skin. My teeth chattered, but I kept going, trying to wash him off me.

A cold panic seized me. This. This was the trap. The quiet breathing, the shared heat, the way my fingers had found his in the dark. This was the connection I'd been running from, and it had found me in my sleep.

This is how it starts. You get comfortable. You start to need them.

I gripped the sink, staring at my reflection.

And then they leave. They always leave. Dad left. Brandon would have left eventually, once he saw past the perfect daughter act. Everyone leaves when they figure out you're not worth the effort.

Better to push him away now. Better to be the one who ruins it before he can.

When I finally emerged, Wyatt had rebuilt the fire and started coffee on the camp stove. He'd changed his shirt, pulled on a heavier sweater. We moved around each other in careful choreography, maintaining a buffer of space that felt louder than words.

"Storm's easing up." He stared out the window instead of at me. "Radio says maybe another day."

"Good." I grabbed a mug, poured coffee with hands that wanted to shake. "That's good."

The day stretched between us like a tightrope. We ate breakfast in shifts—him by the window, me curled in the chair farthest from where we'd slept. I tried to write but kept finding myself staring at the same sentence. He went through the motions of checking supplies, securing loose boards, anything that kept his hands busy and his back to me.

The silence wasn't empty; it was sharp. The scrape of his fork on his plate was a physical jolt. The rustle of my notebook pages sounded like a scream. Every small sound had teeth, tearing at the space between us.

By evening, I couldn't stand it anymore. Movement meant purpose, so I started dinner with our dwindling supplies. A can of soup, the last of the stale bread, some cheese that had seen better days. The cold metal of the can opener bit into my palm. My hands shook, and the tool's gear slipped against the can's rim with a useless scrape. I reset it, my jaw tight, focusing on the simple, mechanical task as if it were the only thing holding me together.

"Let me help." Wyatt appeared at my elbow, reaching for the opener.

"I don't need rescuing." The words came out sharper than intended, edged with something that had nothing to do with soup.

He stepped back, hands raised slightly. "Never said you did."

That patient tone, like he was gentling a spooked horse, made everything worse. I turned back to the soup, managed to get the can open without further incident. The silence stretched while I heated it on the camp stove, stirring with more focus than cream of mushroom required.

"I need to know."

His voice cut through the quiet like an axe through wood. I kept stirring.

"Was it just the schedule? The running, the firefighting, the never staying in one place?" He moved into my peripheral vision, leaning against the counter. "Or was there someone else?"

The spoon slipped from my fingers, clattering against the pot. My hands gripped the counter edge until my knuckles went white.

"There was someone else."

The words fell into the space between us like stones into deep water. I couldn't look at him, but I felt the change in the air, the way he went still.

"Right." His voice had gone flat, emotionless. "I guess that—"

"I was engaged. When I met you."

Silence. Complete, deafening silence that pressed against my eardrums. The soup bubbled on the stove, little volcanic bursts that seemed obscenely cheerful.

I forced myself to turn, to face him. His expression had gone blank, that careful nothing that was worse than anger or hurt or disgust. Just... nothing.

"His name was Brandon." The words tumbled out, rushing to fill the vacuum. "Six months engaged. My mother adored him. Partner at a law firm, stable, safe, everything she wanted for me."

Wyatt hadn't moved. Hadn't even blinked.

"I went to Portland for that conference. Just a weekend away, nothing special. Brandon was supposed to come but canceled last minute. Some deposition he couldn't miss." My laugh came out broken. "I was relieved. That should have told me everything, but I was too much of a coward to see it."

The soup started to burn. I turned off the burner, the mundane action steadying me enough to continue.

"Then I met you." My voice dropped, barely audible over the storm. "And everything I thought I knew about myself, about what I wanted, about what feeling alive meant—it all just... shattered."

I pressed my palms against my eyes, trying to hold back the tears that wanted to fall.

"Three days. Three impossible days where I felt more myself than I had in years. You made me laugh. Really laugh, not the polite sound I'd perfected for dinner parties. You listened when I talked about writing like it mattered, like I mattered. You looked at me like I was someone worth looking at."

I dropped my hands, forced myself to meet his eyes.

"Being with Brandon was a prison sentence. Every day was another role to play—the dutiful fiancée, the perfect daughter-in-law, the woman who smiled at charity galas and never said what she actually thought. I was so good at it, Wyatt. So good at being what everyone expected."

My voice cracked.

"That weekend with you was the first time I ever acted with authenticity. The first time I stopped performing and just... was. I know how that sounds. I know it doesn't excuse what I did. But Portland wasn't a betrayal of Brandon—it was the moment I finally stopped lying to myself about what I deserved. It was over I just hadn't said the words to him yet. And when I told him, he was relieved because it wasn't right for him either."

"You weren't wearing a ring."

His voice cut through my rambling, quiet but sharp. I dropped my hands, met his eyes.

"I took it off. That first night, after my friends left. Went to the bathroom and took it off, shoved it in my purse." The shame burned through me, hot and acidic. "I told myself it was just for the weekend. Just a fantasy. Nobody would get hurt."

"And you left. You disappeared without a word."

"I broke up with Brandon the morning I got back." The tears came now, streaming down my face. "Gave him back the ring, and called off everything. It took one hour to dismantle six months of planning."

"Then why—"

"How could I tell you?" The words ripped from my throat. "How could I call you and say, 'Hi, remember that incredible weekend? Remember how we talked about honesty and being real? Well, I was engaged the whole time. But don't worry, I ended it the day after I left you.' How could I say that?"

My legs gave out. I slid down the cabinet until I hit the floor, knees pulled to my chest.

"You were... real. Honest. You fought fires and talked about your brothers and you never seemed to pretend. And I was a liar. A fake. The kind of person who smiles at her fiancé's parents while hiding another man's phone number in her purse." My voice broke completely. "You deserved better. You deserved someone who didn't have to lie to be with you."

I wiped at my face with shaking hands.

"But I'm also telling you this now because I need you to see it. I need you to see exactly who I am—someone who lies, who runs, who ruins good things before they can ruin her. Because this morning, when I woke up in your arms, I felt safe. And that terrifies me more than anything else."

My voice dropped to barely a whisper.

"This is how it starts. You get comfortable. You start to need them. And then they leave. So I'm giving you the reason to leave now, before I need you any more than I already do."

The kitchen went quiet except for my ragged breathing and the wind outside. I couldn't look up, couldn't bear to see disgust or disappointment or whatever had replaced that beautiful blankness on his face.

The floor creaked as he moved. I expected footsteps heading away, the sound of him putting distance between us. Instead, he sank down against the cabinet opposite me, his long legs stretched out parallel to mine.

We sat like that, three feet of linoleum between us that might as well have been an ocean. The soup congealed in its pot. The fire crackled in the other room. And I waited for him to speak, to rage, to leave—anything but this terrible silence that said everything without saying anything at all.

Breaking the Surface

Wyatt

The kitchen floor was cold under my knees. Three feet of cracked linoleum stretched between us—Emma pressed against one cabinet, me against the other. Her shoulders shook with silent sobs. The flannel shirt I'd given her was too big, swallowing her frame, making her look smaller than she was. Fragile.

Engaged.

The word was a shard of ice in my gut. She'd been someone else's when we met. When we laughed over terrible hotel coffee. When we argued about Elizabeth Bennet's choices. When she'd kissed me in that Portland bar like the world was ending and beginning all at once.

The soup pot sat forgotten on the stove, a skin forming on its surface. Outside, the wind had gentled from a howl to a whisper. Even the storm was exhausted.

I watched her curl tighter into herself, a small, broken thing on my kitchen floor. The anger I expected never came. The betrayal I should have felt was nowhere. All I felt was the cold floor under my ass and a sharp, sudden ache in my chest, like I'd just surfaced into air so clean it burned.

She wasn't lying to me. She was lying to herself. She was drowning, and I know what that feels like.

This was the moment everything shifted. Not forgiveness—that implied judgment, and I had no right to judge. This was recognition. She wasn't the woman who ran. She was my equal in fear and damage.

"Emma."

Her head stayed buried against her knees.

"Look at me."

She lifted her face. Tears cut clean paths through the grime on her cheeks. Her eyes were swollen, nose red, bottom lip trembling. Beautiful. Broken. Real.

"I would have chosen you."

Her whole body went rigid. "What?"

"If you'd asked. If you'd told me. If you'd called the next day or the next week or the next month." The words came out steady, each one a stone dropped into still water. "I would have come back to you."

"You don't know that." Her voice cracked on the last word. "You were heading to California. Another fire, another crew, another—"

"I never went to California."

That stopped her cold.

"Changed my mind at the state line. Turned around, took a job in Oregon instead. Spent three months jumping fires forty miles from Portland." My laugh came out rough. "Kept telling myself I'd drive down on a day off. Just to see. Never did."

"Why not?"

"Because you left. No note, no number, no last name I could track down. You vanished like smoke, and I figured that was your answer."

She pressed her palms against her eyes. "I was so ashamed."

"You ended it with him."

"After. After I'd already—" Her breath hitched. "I was the kind of woman who cheats. Who lies. Who—"

"Who was drowning in the wrong life."

The words hung between us. She dropped her hands, staring at me like I'd spoken a foreign language.

"You think I don't recognize drowning when I see it?" I shifted, my back protesting from the hard floor, but I didn't move closer. Not yet. "I've been drowning my whole life, Emma. Different states, different fires, different beds. Never stopping long enough to need oxygen."

Her tears had stopped. She watched me with those green-gold eyes that had haunted five years of restless nights.

"Then I met you. Three days in Portland, and suddenly I could breathe. Actually breathe. Full lungs, clear head, like breaking the surface after being under too long." The confession scraped my throat raw. "You know what terrified me most?"

She shook her head, a tiny movement.

"How easy it was. How right it felt. Like my whole life had been leading to that hotel bar, that argument about Jane Austen, that first kiss that tasted like whiskey and possibility."

"Wyatt—"

"I've been running from that feeling for five years. New crews, new states, new women who never quite fit the shape you left behind." My hands clenched against my thighs. "So don't tell me what I would or wouldn't have chosen. I've been choosing you every day since Portland. I just didn't know if you were choosing me back."

The kitchen settled into silence. The refrigerator hummed. The fire popped in the next room. Emma uncurled slowly, her legs sliding straight, mirroring my position. Our feet almost touched in the middle of the narrow space.

"This doesn't change anything." Her voice was small, defeated. "You're still leaving for Montana."

"In six weeks."

"And I'm going back to Seattle."

"After Christmas."

"So what's the point? Why do this to ourselves again?"

I pushed myself to standing, every muscle protesting from the night on the hard floor. Emma tracked my movement, chin lifting as I stood over her. I extended my hand.

She stared at it like it might bite. "Wyatt—"

"Take my hand, Emma."

"Why?"

"Because I'm tired of having this conversation on the floor."

Her fingers slid into mine, warm despite everything. I pulled her up slowly, steadying her when she swayed. We stood in the tiny kitchen, bodies inches apart, hands still linked.

"You weren't a coward." My free hand came up, thumb brushing the tear tracks on her cheek. "You made the hard choice. Broke it off. Did the right thing."

"Too late though." The words were barely a breath.

"Maybe not."

Her eyes searched mine, looking for something—hope, possibility, promise. I leaned closer. It wasn't a choice. It was just... happening. The way it happened in Portland. Her lips parted. Her breath feathered across my mouth.

"You're still leaving." The whisper shattered the moment like dropped glass. "Montana in six weeks."

Reality crashed back in, cold as the storm outside. I pulled back, dropped her hand, stepped away until my back hit the counter.

"Right. Yeah."

She wrapped her arms around herself, that defensive curl returning. "I should—the soup's ruined. I'll make something else."

"I'm not hungry."

"We should eat something."

"Emma—"

"Please." Her voice broke on the word. "Just. Please."

I left her in the kitchen, rebuilding her walls pot by pot, can by can.

Worth the Wait

♥

Wyatt

The fire had burned low again by morning. I'd fed it through the night, unable to sleep, watching the flames dance while Emma curled in the chair across the room. Neither of us had attempted the floor again.

Gray light filtered through the windows, revealing a world buried in white. The storm had exhausted itself, leaving only occasional gusts that rattled the windows like afterthoughts.

Day five. Rescue would come soon. Tomorrow, maybe today if the plows worked fast. Then back to reality. Back to separate lives and opposite directions.

Emma emerged from her chair like a cat, all careful stretches and defensive posture. Her hair was a disaster, red-gold tangles that my fingers itched to smooth. She'd never looked more beautiful or more unreachable.

"Coffee?" Her voice was carefully neutral, the tone she'd used that first day when she'd answered the door expecting anyone but me.

"Yeah."

We moved through the morning routine like swimmers underwater—slow, deliberate, maintaining careful distance. Coffee on the camp stove. Last of the powdered eggs. Stale bread toasted over the fire. Neither of us ate much.

"Radio says the roads—" she started.

"I know."

Silence settled between us, heavy as the snow outside. I stood by the window, watching nothing, seeing everything—five years of empty beds, empty roads, empty choices. She sat in her chair, notebook open but pen still, staring at the fire. A single tear escaped, tracing a clean path through the grime on her cheek.

And that was it. The sight of that one tear broke whatever restraint I had left. Five years of running, five days of silence—gone.

I crossed the room in three strides. Emma looked up, startled, as I pulled her from the chair. The notebook tumbled to the floor.

"What are you—"

"I'm tired of pretending I don't want this."

Her hands came up, pressing against my chest. "We can't. You're leaving. I'm leaving. This is just cabin fever, just proximity—"

"Bullshit."

"Wyatt—"

"I don't care." My hands framed her face, forcing her to meet my eyes. "Six weeks, six days, six hours. I don't care. I want whatever time we have."

"That's not—we can't just—"

I kissed her again, slower this time, deeper. My hands slid beneath the hem of the flannel—*my* flannel, the one she'd stolen from my bag the first night—and found the warm, smooth skin of her waist. She gasped into my mouth when my thumbs brushed the undersides of her breasts, her nipples already tight beneath the thin fabric of her tank top.

"Wyatt—" Her voice was rough, her fingers digging into my shoulders like she was afraid I'd disappear.

"Tell me to stop," I challenged, my mouth trailing down her throat. She tasted like salt and need, her pulse hammering against my lips. "Tell me this isn't what you've wanted since we saw each other at the engagement party."

She didn't. Instead, she arched into me, her breath hitching when I bit down gently on the sensitive spot where her neck met her shoulder. The sound she made—half moan, half whimper—went straight to my cock, already hard and aching against the zipper of my jeans.

Her hands dropped between us, fumbling with my belt. "I *hate* you for this."

I laughed, low and dark, catching her wrist and pressing her palm against the bulge in my jeans. "No, you don't."

She swallowed, her thighs clamping around mine as I rolled my hips up, letting her feel exactly what she did to me. "God, I *hate* that you're right."

The flannel hit the floor. Then her tank top, tossed aside like it was on fire. She wasn't wearing a bra. Five years, and she still slept like this—bare beneath her clothes, like she trusted the world not to see her. Like she'd been waiting for *me* to see her.

I groaned, my hands covering her breasts, thumbs circling her nipples until they were dark pink and pebbled. "Fuck, Emma."

She whimpered, her head falling back as I leaned in, taking one tight peak into my mouth. Her fingers tangled in my hair, holding me there as I laved and sucked, my free hand sliding down to grip her thigh, urging her to rock against me. The friction was maddening—denim against denim, the heat of her through the layers of clothing we wore.

"Not fair," she gasped, her hips moving in desperate little circles. "You're still dressed."

I released her with a wet pop, my breath ragged. "Fix that."

She didn't hesitate. Her fingers flew over the buttons of my shirt, shoving it off my shoulders before attacking my belt. I kicked off my boots, my jeans, my boxers—everything, until I was bare beneath her, my cock jutting up between us, thick and flushed.

Emma stilled, her gaze locked on me. Then, slowly, she reached out, her fingers wrapping around my length. I hissed, my hips jerking into her touch.

"Still the same," she murmured, stroking me from root to tip, her thumb swiping over the precome beading at the slit. "Still *perfect*."

I growled, my control snapping. In one move, I flipped her onto her back, pinning her wrists above her head. "My turn."

Her jeans were gone in a second, torn down her legs, her underwear following. And then—*fuck*—she was naked beneath me, spread open, glistening and swollen and so goddamn *beautiful* it hurt.

I didn't give her time to think. I dropped my head between her thighs, my tongue dragging through her folds in one long, slow lick. She cried out, her back arching off the couch, her fingers clawing at the cushions.

"Wyatt—*please*—"

I groaned against her, the taste of her—sweet, musky, *hers*—making my head spin. I feasted on her, my tongue circling her clit before sucking it between my lips, my fingers pressing inside her, curling until I found the spot that made her legs shake.

"Don't stop—*don't stop*—" Her voice was broken, her hips bucking against my mouth. I added another finger, stretching her, preparing her, my free hand gripping her hip to hold her still as I devoured her.

When she came, it was with a choked sob, her thighs clamping around my head, her release flooding my tongue. I lapped at her through it, prolonging every shudder, every gasp, until she was boneless beneath me.

I crawled up her body, my cock dragging through her wetness, both of us groaning at the contact.

"Condom," she managed, her voice slurred with pleasure.

I didn't want to leave her. Didn't want to break this spell. But I forced myself to reach for my discarded jeans, tearing the foil packet open with my teeth. She took it from me, her hands rolling it down my length with excruciating slowness.

Then she was pulling me back to her, her legs wrapping around my waist, her heels digging into my ass. "Now, Wyatt. *Now.*"

I didn't need to be told twice.

I thrust into her in one deep, claiming stroke, burying myself to the hilt. We both cried out—her from the stretch, the fullness, me from the sheer *rightness* of it, the way her body gripped me like she'd been made for me.

"Fuck," I groaned, my forehead pressing to hers. "Emma—*fuck*—"

She kissed me, her tongue tangling with mine as I began to move, slow at first, then harder, deeper, the couch creaking beneath us. Every thrust was punctuated by the wet, obscene sound of our bodies coming together, the slap of skin, the ragged sounds tearing from her throat.

"More," she demanded, her nails raking down my back. "I want *all* of you."

I gave it to her.

I flipped her onto her hands and knees, my hands gripping her hips as I drove into her from behind, watching the way her ass jiggled with every snap of my hips, the way her spine arched, the way she reached back to touch herself, her fingers circling her clit as I fucked her like I'd dreamed of for years.

"Like that?" I growled, "You want me to take you like this? Make you scream so loud the whole mountain hears?"

"Yes—*yes*—" Her voice was a broken whisper, her body tightening around me. "I'm close—I'm *so close*—"

I reached around, my fingers replacing hers, rubbing her clit in tight, relentless circles as I pounded into her. "Come for me, Emma."

She shattered with a cry, her body clamping down around me like a vise, her release milking me over the edge. I buried myself deep and came with a groan, my cock pulsing inside her as waves of pleasure wrecked me, my vision whiting out, my grip on her hips bruising.

We collapsed onto the couch, a tangle of limbs and ragged breaths, my cock still buried inside her, neither of us willing to break the connection.

Emma turned her head, her lips finding mine in a slow, lazy kiss. "That was—"

"Five years in the making," I finished, brushing a damp strand of hair from her forehead.

She laughed softly, her body still trembling around me. "Worth the wait."

I pulled her closer, my arms locking around her like I could keep her here forever. "Yeah. It was."

Outside, the storm raged on. But in that moment, with her in my arms, the world could have ended, and I wouldn't have cared.

After, we lay tangled on the too-narrow couch, her head on my chest, my arms locked around her like I could keep her through pure will.

"This doesn't change anything." Her voice was soft, sad, satisfied.

"I know."

"You're still leaving."

I didn't answer. Couldn't. The weight of that truth sat on my chest heavier than her body.

"But we have today," she continued. "And tonight. And however long until the plows come."

The rest of the day passed in a haze of touch and talk and the kind of comfortable silence that usually takes years to build. We cooked together—the last of our supplies turned into something approaching edible. We talked about nothing—books, movies, the proper way to build a fire. We didn't talk about tomorrow.

She curled against me on the couch, wearing my sweater now, reading from her notebook while I played with her hair.

"It's terrible," she said about her writing. "The characters are all wrong."

"Read me some."

"Absolutely not."

"Come on. I showed you my scars."

"That's different."

"How?"

She was quiet for a moment. "Because your scars healed. These words are still bleeding."

I kissed the top of her head. "Then let me help stop the bleeding."

She read me a paragraph—something about a male firefighter afraid to love again. The words were beautiful, painful, clearly autobiographical.

"She should trust him," I said when she finished.

"Even though he's leaving?"

"Maybe he's not. Maybe he's waiting for her to ask him to stay."

Emma set the notebook aside, turned in my arms to face me. "Is that what you're doing? Waiting for me to ask?"

"I don't know what I'm doing. For the first time in my life, I have no idea what comes next."

"That terrifies you."

"Yes."

"Me too."

We sat with that truth between us, heavy as the snow outside.

"Tell me something you've never told anyone," I said, needing to lighten the weight.

She considered. "I kept your number. All five years. In my phone, unnamed, just ten digits I couldn't bring myself to delete."

"Why unnamed?"

"Because naming you made you real. And if you were real, then leaving you was real. And that was too much to carry."

My chest cracked wider. "I looked you up. It took awhile, but I managed. Found your LinkedIn, your Instagram. Never messaged, never called."

"Why not?"

"Pride. Fear. Take your pick." I traced patterns on her arm, nonsense designs that somehow made sense. "Mac—my jump partner—he said I was an idiot. Said any woman worth remembering after three days was worth fighting for."

"Smart man."

"Smarter than me."

"What else did he say?"

"That I was using fire to run from getting burned." My laugh came out rough. "Twelve years of therapy in one drunk conversation."

Emma pulled back enough to study my face. "We're both so broken."

"Yeah."

"And scared."

"Terrified."

"And this is probably the worst idea either of us has ever had."

"Definitely."

She kissed me anyway, slow and deep and full of all the words we couldn't say. When we finally broke apart, the light outside was fading, the fire burning low.

"We should add more wood," she said against my mouth.

"We should do a lot of things."

Neither of us moved.

"Tell me about Montana," she said finally. "The job."

"It's a good position. Permanent crew leader spot. Benefits, stability, all the things I've been avoiding."

"But?"

"But it's Montana."

"And?"

"And you're here."

"I'm not here. Not really. This is just a rental, a summer that's turned into fall. I belong in Seattle."

"Do you?"

She didn't answer.

We built up the fire together, moving in easy synchronization. She handed me logs, I placed them. She adjusted the damper, I added kindling. Five days and we'd learned each other's rhythms, the dance of shared space.

"What if—" she started, then stopped.

"What?"

"Nothing. It's stupid."

"Tell me anyway."

"What if we just had this? These days, this bubble, this perfect impossibility?"

"And then?"

"And then we go back to our lives. You to Montana, me to Seattle. We store this away like those three days in Portland—perfect because they ended."

"That's not enough."

"It has to be."

"Emma—"

"I can't ask you to stay. You'd resent me. And I can't follow you to Montana. I'd lose myself." Her voice broke on the last word. "So we take what we can get."

I wanted to argue, to promise things I couldn't deliver, to swear I'd never resent her or leave her or disappoint her. But the words stuck in my throat, trapped by twenty years of learned behavior, of watching Mason sacrifice everything, of running before anyone could ask me to stop.

So I pulled her close instead, buried my face in her hair, and tried to memorize everything—the smell of woodsmoke in her hair, the way she fit against me, the sound of her heartbeat gradually syncing with mine.

Outside, the wind picked up again, not a storm but a whisper. Inside, we held each other and pretended tomorrow would never come.

The Flannel of Choice

♥

Emma

I traced the grain of the wood with my eyes, counting knots and whorls while his breathing evened out against my shoulder. Five days trapped in this cabin, and I'd memorized every beam, every imperfection in the walls. Tomorrow the plows would come. Tomorrow this ended.

His arm tightened around my waist, pulling me closer against his chest. The heat of his skin burned through the thin cotton of his t-shirt I'd stolen. Outside, the wind had finally quieted to a whisper. No more howling. No more snow battering the windows. Just the soft creak of settling wood and our matched breathing.

"What if I stayed?"

The words dropped into the darkness between us. My heart stuttered, then hammered against my ribs hard enough that he had to feel it.

"What?" I turned in his arms, searching for his face in the dim light filtering up from the dying fire below.

"In Copper Ridge." His fingers found my hair, winding through the tangles. "What if I didn't go to Montana?"

A breath I didn't know I was holding escaped in a sharp hiss. I pushed up on one elbow, needing to see his expression. His gray eyes caught what little light there was, but I couldn't read them.

"What about the job? The permanent position?"

"There are other jobs." His hand moved to my cheek, thumb brushing along my cheekbone. "Mason's always saying they need experienced guys at the station. Cole can't handle all the medical calls alone."

My chest expanded with something dangerous. Hope. It filled me like helium, lifting me up, making me dizzy.

"You'd really do that?" My voice came out small, vulnerable in a way that scared me. "Give up Montana?"

His thumb stilled on my cheek. A muscle in his jaw twitched.

"I mean, it was only a thought." The words came faster now, tumbling over each other. "Montana's a really good position. Benefits, stability. The crew there is top-notch."

There. Right there. The flash of panic that flared in his eyes, there and gone before I could name it. I saw it clear as if he'd written it across his forehead: *What am I saying? What am I promising?*

I knew it.

The thought came sharp and cold, cutting through the hope like a blade through tissue paper. Of course. Of course this was happening. I'd let myself believe—for five days, for a handful of hours in his arms—that maybe this time would be different. That maybe I was different. Worth staying for.

But this was the part I knew by heart. The script I'd memorized from my father and from every man who'd ever looked at me with want but not enough want. This was the moment right before they left. The panic. The backpedaling. The careful extraction.

I let myself hope, and this is what happens.

The hope in my chest curdled, turned heavy as wet cement. I forced my lips into what might pass for a smile in the dark.

"Right. Of course."

"Emma—"

"Let's enjoy this while we have it." I lay back down, careful not to touch him even though we were sharing a space barely wide enough for one person, let alone two. "No point making plans we won't keep."

This is the part where he leaves.

Not tonight. Maybe not tomorrow. But soon. They always did. And I'd known it—had known it from the moment I opened the cabin door and saw him standing there with his gray eyes and his temporary life. I'd known it, and I'd let him in anyway.

Stupid. So stupid.

The only sound was wood creaking as the cabin settled around us. Even Wyatt's breathing had gone quiet, a careful, measured rhythm that felt miles away. I held my own breath, counting the seconds between his inhales, aware of the inch of cold air that now separated his back from mine.

The radio crackled from downstairs, shattering the quiet.

"...National Weather Service update. Storm system moving east. Temperatures rising overnight. Road crews scheduled to begin clearing operations at dawn. Highway 34 expected to reopen by noon..."

The mechanical voice droned on with wind speeds and precipitation totals, but all I heard was the countdown. Dawn. Noon. Hours, not days.

Wyatt's hand found mine in the dark, fingers lacing through mine. His palm was rough, calloused from years of handling equipment, fighting fires, saving everyone but himself from burning.

"Emma, I—"

"I know." I squeezed his fingers once, then pulled my hand away. "We both knew this was temporary."

We lay there, both staring at the ceiling. The fire popped downstairs, sending shadows dancing across the loft. My novel manuscript sat on the desk by the window, sixty thousand words of a love story I couldn't figure out how to end. Just like us.

Sleep wasn't coming. Every time I closed my eyes, I saw that flash of panic in his. The moment he realized what staying would mean. Commitment. Roots. All the things Wyatt Drake had spent thirty-two years avoiding.

I slid from the couch, the movement slow, careful not to disturb him.

The fire was a weak pulse of orange in the hearth, offering no warmth at all. I snatched the wool blanket from the couch, wrapped it around my shoulders, and settled at my makeshift desk.

The notebook fell open. Her asking him to stay. Him unable to answer. My own life, bleeding onto the page. I picked up the pen.

She knew before he spoke that he was already gone. Not physically—he was right there, warm and solid beside her. But the important parts of him, the parts that might have chosen her, had already packed their bags.

The words flowed fast, my handwriting getting messier with each line. An alternate ending. One where fear won. Where patterns held. Where people were who they'd always been and love wasn't enough to change them.

"Can't sleep?"

I didn't turn around. Wyatt's voice came from the couch, rough with exhaustion or something else.

"Had an idea. Didn't want to lose it."

The couch creaked. He was giving me space, sitting near but not too near. The careful distance of someone who didn't know where the boundaries were anymore.

"What kind of idea?"

I kept writing, pen scratching across paper. "An alternative ending. Where they both choose fear instead of each other."

"That's depressing."

I set down the pen, the scratching sound ending abruptly. My gaze lifted to find him. He stood by the dying fire in just his jeans, arms crossed over his bare chest. The firelight turned his skin gold, threw shadows under his ribs. Beautiful and temporary, like everything else about these five days.

"Maybe. Or maybe it's realistic."

He studied me for a long moment, and I could see him weighing words, discarding responses. The Wyatt from three hours ago would have argued, would have kissed me to prove that fear didn't have to win. This Wyatt, the one who'd panicked at his own suggestion of staying, just nodded.

"How does it end? Your alternative."

I looked back at my notebook.

"She lets him go. He leaves for his next job, next fire, next reason to keep moving. She goes back to her life in the city. They both tell themselves it's for the best."

"Do they believe it?"

"Does it matter if they do?"

He moved then, came to stand behind my chair. Not touching, just there, reading over my shoulder. His breath stirred my hair.

"That's not how it should end."

"No?" I picked up the pen again, added another line. *He kissed her goodbye at the door, and they both pretended it didn't feel like dying.* "How should it end then?"

Silence. Then his hand on my shoulder, warm through the blanket.

"I don't know."

The honest answer. The only answer he could give. I covered his hand with mine, just for a moment, then pulled away.

"The roads will be clear soon."

"Yeah."

"You should sleep. Long drive to Montana."

"I'm not leaving tomorrow. Not directly anyway. Need to help with storm cleanup, check in with Mason."

"But eventually."

"Eventually."

The word hung between us, heavy with all its implications. Eventually he'd leave. Eventually I'd go back to Seattle. Eventually we'd be strangers again, just two people who'd shared five days in a snowstorm and learned exactly why they couldn't be together.

I closed the notebook, stood up. The blanket fell from my shoulders, pooling on the floor. We faced each other in the dying firelight, and I could see everything in his eyes—want and fear and the terrible knowledge that he couldn't be who I needed him to be.

"Come back to bed." His voice was rough. "We still have tonight."

I wanted to say no. To protect what was left of my heart by starting the separation now. But his hand reached for mine, and I was weak, had always been weak when it came to him.

"Just tonight."

We lay down carefully, formally, like strangers sharing a too-small space. But in the dark, his arm found its way around me. My head found his shoulder. Our breathing synced without thought.

"I'm sorry," he whispered into my hair.

"For what?"

"For being who you knew I was."

I pressed my face into his chest, breathed him in—smoke and pine and the particular scent that was just Wyatt.

"I'm sorry too."

"For what?"

"For hoping you weren't."

The radio crackled again. More weather updates. Road conditions improving. Life returning to normal. The storm was over.

We held each other in the dark and pretended morning would never come.

The False High

♥

Wyatt

The rumble started low, distant—diesel engines grinding through snow. I jerked awake, the sound yanking me from dreams I couldn't quite remember but that left my chest aching. Emma stirred against me, her hand tightening on my shirt for just a second before she went rigid.

The plows. They'd made it up the mountain.

Neither of us moved. Her breath warmed the hollow of my throat. My arm was still around her waist, fingers spread across her hip.

The engines grew louder. Multiple vehicles. Voices carried on the cold air.

Emma pulled away first, the loss of her warmth immediate and sharp. She sat up, not looking at me, and started finger-combing her hair into something presentable. The morning light streaming through the window turned her skin pale, washed out the color in her cheeks.

"So." Her voice came out rough.

"Yeah."

I swung my legs over the edge of the couch, grabbed my jeans from the floor. The denim was cold, stiff. Everything felt wrong—too bright, too loud, too real after the soft darkness we'd been living in.

Emma stood first. I followed, watching her shoulders set into that careful posture I recognized from the wedding. Armor going up, brick by brick.

She moved around the cabin with mechanical precision—folding the blanket we'd wrapped ourselves in last night, stacking the books we'd read to each other, straightening cushions that didn't need straightening. Her hands shook, just barely, as she smoothed the fabric.

"Emma—"

"Your boots are by the door." She didn't turn around.

I pulled them on, the laces stiff with cold. Outside, the trucks were close now. Mason's voice cut through the engine noise, giving directions to someone. Lily's higher tone followed, worried, asking questions I couldn't make out.

Emma twisted her hair into a knot, securing it with an elastic from her wrist. She'd stolen my t-shirt at some point, wore it under her cardigan. The hem hung past her hips, and something in my chest twisted at the sight.

"You should probably..." She gestured vaguely at my general dishevelment.

I ran a hand through my hair, achieving nothing. Five days of stubble scratched my palm. My flannel was wrinkled beyond salvation, and I probably smelled like—

"Wyatt! Emma! You in there?"

Mason. Of course he'd be first on scene, making sure everyone was accounted for. Making sure I hadn't done something stupid.

Too late for that.

Emma's hand hovered over the door handle. She looked at me once, and I saw everything in that glance—regret, hurt, the careful distance she was already putting between us.

She opened the door.

Mason walked to the porch in his chief's jacket, Lily beside him bundled in enough layers to survive an arctic expedition. Behind them, a county plow truck idled, the driver leaning out his window to watch.

Lily's eyes darted between Emma and me, reading the situation in about three seconds flat. Her mouth tightened.

Mason's expression went from concerned to stone. His gaze traveled from my wrinkled clothes to Emma's defensive posture to the careful space between us.

"Everyone okay?" His tone suggested he already knew the answer.

"Fine." Emma's voice was too bright. "The generator died, but we managed with the fireplace."

"Roads are clear back to town." The plow driver called out. "Should stay that way if this weather holds."

"Thank you." Emma moved past Mason and Lily onto the porch, wrapping her arms around herself against the cold.

Lily followed immediately. "Let me help you check for any damage. That wind was brutal."

They disappeared around the side of the cabin, Lily's hand on Emma's lower back, guiding her away. Emma didn't look back.

Mason waited until they were out of earshot, then crossed his arms. The universal Drake stance for 'we need to talk.'

"Generator's completely fried." I grabbed the first topic that might deflect him. "Emma's lucky she had enough firewood. She could've—"

"Cut the crap."

"I should check the roof. Make sure no shingles—"

"Wyatt."

I stopped, shoulders dropping. No point pretending. Mason had been reading me since I was thirteen and trying to hide stolen beer behind the shed.

"You look like hell."

"Thanks."

"What did you do?" Mason's voice was low, each word a piece of gravel.

The question landed like a punch. Not 'what happened.' Just blame.

"Nothing," I bit out, shoving my hands in my pockets. "We got snowed in. Kept the fire going."

He just stared, his silence more damning than any accusation. Finally, I cracked. "Fine. What do you want me to say? We slept together. It happened. It's over."

"Is it?"

"I leave for Montana in six weeks, Mase. You know the plan."

"Plans change."

"Not this one." I looked past him, at the tracks in the snow leading away from the cabin. "I'm not you."

That hit him. I saw it in the tightening of his jaw. "What the hell is that supposed to mean?"

"It means I saw what you gave up. College. Your twenties. Everything. I'm not doing that to her. I won't be the reason she's stuck here, and I won't be the reason I am either."

His voice dropped, the anger replaced by something raw. "You think I feel stuck? You think raising you and James was a sacrifice I regret?"

"Wasn't it?"

"Jesus, Wyatt." He scrubbed a hand over his face. "That wasn't a job. That was my family. There's a difference. One you're apparently too scared to figure out."

Through the window, I could see Emma and Lily by the woodpile. Emma's shoulders were shaking—crying or laughing, I couldn't tell. Lily had an arm around her, but Emma stood rigid, separate.

"She's in love with you." Mason said it like stating a fact about weather patterns or fire behavior.

"She's in love with the idea of me staying. There's a difference."

"Is there? Or are you just too scared to find out?"

Inside the cabin, voices drifted from the back room.

"I'm an idiot." Emma's voice, muffled but clear enough. "I knew better and I did it anyway."

"Hey." Lily's tone was gentle. "You're not an idiot. You're human."

"Same thing, apparently."

"Did you tell him how you feel?"

A long pause. When Emma spoke again, her voice was smaller. "What's the point? He's leaving in six weeks."

"Emma—"

"No." Her voice was stronger, but brittle. "I'm not doing this again, Lily. I can't."

"Doing what?" Lily's voice was gentle.

A choked sound. "Waiting. Hoping. It's my father all over again, always waiting for him to choose to stay. And Wyatt... he's just like him. He'll always choose the next fire, the next horizon. I knew that five years ago. I'm an idiot for forgetting."

Each word was a nail driven deep. She'd already decided. Already written us off. And why shouldn't she? I'd shown her who I was—someone who suggested staying and then immediately backtracked. Someone who could love her for five days but couldn't promise six weeks, much less forever.

Mason was still watching me. "You're going to regret this."

"Probably."

"Then why—"

"Because regretting it from Montana is better than destroying it by staying."

The plow driver honked his horn. "I gotta get moving. More roads to clear."

Mason stepped back. "Storm cleanup starts in an hour. I expect you at the station."

"I'll be there."

"And Wyatt?" He paused at the porch steps. "You're wrong. About all of it. But you're going to have to figure that out yourself."

Emma and Lily came back around the cabin. Emma had pulled herself together, face calm, eyes dry. She moved past me into the cabin without acknowledgment, like I was furniture.

"I'll follow you down." Lily told Mason. "Just let me help Emma get her things together."

They all assumed she was leaving. Going back to town, back to pretending these five days hadn't happened. And from the way Emma was pulling her laptop into her bag, checking for phone chargers, gathering the scattered pages of her manuscript, they were right.

I stood on the porch, useless, watching her erase evidence of us. The coffee mug I'd used sat by the sink. She washed it, dried it, put it away. The blanket we'd shared was folded with military precision. Even the indent in the couch cushion where we'd spent hours wrapped around each other got fluffed back to neutral.

"Your jacket." She held out my heavy winter coat without looking at me.

I took it. Our fingers didn't touch.

Mason started his truck, the diesel engine loud in the morning qui-et. Lily carried Emma's laptop bag to her SUV while Emma did a final check of the cabin. Professional. Thorough. Like she was checking out of a hotel.

"The generator will need to be replaced before the next storm." She said it to the air between us. "I'll let Dorothy know."

"Emma—"

"I should go. Lily's waiting."

She stepped past me, careful not to touch. But I caught her scent—my shirt on her skin, woodsmoke in her hair, that particular perfume of the last five days.

"This isn't over." The words escaped before I could stop them.

She stopped on the top step, her back to me. "Yes, it is. You decided that last night when you couldn't even pretend to mean it."

"That's not—"

"Six weeks, Wyatt. You leave in six weeks. I leave in four. We both knew this was temporary." She turned just enough that I could see her profile. "At least we're being honest about it."

She walked to her SUV, boots crunching through snow. Got in. Started the engine. Lily's vehicle followed hers down the mountain road, leaving deep tracks in the fresh snow.

I stood on the porch until both vehicles disappeared around the bend, until the sound of engines faded, until even the birds went quiet.

The air in the cabin was dead. Stale. The scent of her was already fading, replaced by cold wood and emptiness. I grabbed my snowmobile keys from the table, slammed the door behind me, the sound swallowed by the silence. The lock clicked with a finality that echoed in my chest.

Storm cleanup. Manning the station. Pretending everything was normal while the ghost of Emma's warmth still clung to my shirt.

Six weeks until Montana.

Four weeks until she left.

We'd both made our choices, fallen back into our safe, familiar patterns. She'd stop chasing. I'd keep running.

Everyone would get exactly what they expected.

December 27th

♥

Emma

The cursor blinked at me. Three seconds on, three seconds off. A digital heartbeat mocking my inability to type a single word.

Chapter 22: The Choice

That's all I had. A title and twenty-three blank pages waiting for resolution. My heroes frozen mid-argument for the past twelve days. Every time I tried to write their reconciliation, my fingers seized up over the keyboard.

Coffee had gone cold again. Third cup this morning, or maybe fourth. They all tasted the same now—bitter, necessary, joyless. I pushed the mug aside and rubbed my eyes under my glasses. The cabin's silence pressed against my eardrums, broken only by the wood stove's occasional pop.

My phone buzzed against the desk.

I didn't look. Didn't need to. Same time every morning for two weeks. One text from Wyatt, arriving with the reliability of sunrise.

Yesterday's had flashed on the preview screen: *Emma, we need to talk about—*. My thumb had stabbed the screen, dismissing it before the sentence could finish.

The day before: *I know you're getting these. Please just—*

Delete.

Before that: *I'm sorry about what I said. Can we—*

Delete. Delete. Delete.

The phone went dark again. I stared at the manuscript, at his last line of dialogue suspended in time: "What if I can't be who you need me to be?"

Her response should come next. Something about love being worth the risk, about choosing each other despite their fears. The words were there, I knew they were, but my own thoughts were a wall of static I couldn't tune out.

Tires crunched on the gravel drive.

My heart kicked hard before settling. Lily's Subaru, not Wyatt's truck. I recognized the engine's particular whine, the way she always parked slightly crooked.

The knock came quick and light. "Emma? I brought groceries."

I opened the door to find Lily balancing two paper bags, her breath clouding in the November air. She pushed past me without invitation, heading straight for the kitchen.

"You look terrible." She unpacked eggs, bread, the good coffee from that place in Ridgeway. "When's the last time you ate actual food?"

"I eat."

"Crackers don't count." A carton of soup landed on the counter. "Neither does wine."

She'd seen the empty bottles by the recycling bin. Of course she had.

"I'm fine, Lily."

"Sure you are. That's why you haven't left this cabin in five days." She folded the paper bags with precise creases. "That's why you're wearing the same sweater I saw you in last week."

I glanced down. She was right. Wyatt's shirt underneath it too, though she couldn't see that. I'd meant to wash it, pack it away with everything else from those five days. Instead, I slept in it every night, waking up surrounded by the ghost of woodsmoke and pine.

"I'm working." I gestured at my laptop. "The manuscript is due—"

Lily settled at my small dining table, her coat still on. "So what's really going on?"

"Nothing. I'm just focused on—"

"He's taking every dangerous assignment that comes through dispatch."

The words landed like ice water. I kept my face neutral, busied myself putting groceries away.

"Ridge rescue yesterday in whiteout conditions. Structure fire the night before—went in alone before backup arrived." Lily's voice stayed conversational. "Mason had to pull rank to stop him from rappelling into an unstable mine shaft looking for a dog that turned out to be safe at home." The casual way she said it was its own judgment.

"I don't want to hear about Wyatt."

"Too bad. Someone needs to talk sense into one of you."

"There's no 'us,' Lily. There never really was."

"Five days in that storm say otherwise."

I slammed the refrigerator door, the sound cracking through the cabin's quiet. "Five days of proximity and desperation. That's not real life."

"Felt pretty real when you came back that morning. You looked wrecked, Emma. Both of you did."

"Exactly. Wrecked. That's what we do to each other."

Lily studied me with those dark eyes that missed nothing. "What's your plan here? Hide until spring?"

"No." The word came out too fast. "Actually, I'm leaving."

Her eyebrows rose.

"I booked a flight to Seattle. December 27th."

"The week after Christmas." Lily's voice went flat. "You're really going to run."

"I'm going home."

"This is home. You've been here since May. You extended your rental twice. You have friends here. People who care about—"

"I can't watch him leave." The admission tore from my throat. "In five weeks, he'll pack that truck and drive to Montana, and I'll still be here, pretending it doesn't gut me. I can't, Lily. I barely survived it the first time."

"The first time?"

I sank into the chair across from her. "Five years ago. Portland. We had a long weekend that felt like a lifetime." I pulled my sleeves down over my hands, needing something to hold onto. "I was with Brandon then. Safe, stable Brandon—everything my father wasn't. We'd been together two years, engaged for six months. Wedding planned for that fall. My whole life was algorithms and predictability. A sterile world where nothing unexpected could hurt me."

"Then I met Wyatt at that conference, and it was like—" I searched for the right words. "Like I'd been drowning in shallow water and didn't even know it. Three days with him, and I could finally breathe. Sunday night, he told me about his next assignment—Alaska, nine months. I watched him pack his bag, talking about all the places he'd see, the fires he'd fight. So excited to leave. And I knew that's who he was. Someone who left. But more than that, I knew I wasn't worth staying for. How could I be? I was engaged to someone else. I was a liar and a cheat, and he'd figure that out eventually."

"But you left. Not him."

"The morning I got back to Seattle, I ended it with Brandon. Gave him his ring back before I'd even unpacked. He deserved better than a lie, better than someone going through the motions. I dismantled my entire safe life in one conversation because I couldn't live in that sterile world anymore, couldn't pretend Wyatt hadn't shown me what drowning felt like."

"So you broke it off with Brandon?"

"Immediately. But I couldn't face Wyatt after that. How could I? 'Hey, I was engaged the whole time we were together, but don't worry, I ended it the second I got home.' He'd have thought I was either a cheater or insane. And the worst part? I believed I wasn't worth the chaos. That weekend felt like a backdraft—beautiful and destructive and life-saving all at once. But I convinced myself it was just survival instinct, not something real. Not something worth his staying for."

I stood, needing distance. "I thought maybe this time would be different. But that night in the storm, when he talked about staying, I saw the panic in his eyes. He can't do it. And I can't ask him to be someone he's not."

"Have you tried talking to him?"

"He texts every day."

"And?"

"And I delete them." I moved to the window, watching snow start to fall again. "What's the point? To hear him apologize for being exactly who I knew he was?"

Lily stood, yanking her coat from the back of the chair. "You're both idiots."

"Thanks for the pep talk."

"I'm serious. You're so busy protecting yourselves from getting hurt that you're guaranteeing you will." She paused at the door. "He asks about you. Every day. What you're doing, if you're okay, when you're coming back to town."

"Don't tell him about Seattle."

"I won't. But Emma?" She looked back. "Running doesn't make you brave. It just makes you alone."

The door closed with a soft click. I stood at the window, watching her taillights disappear down the mountain road. Snow kept falling, lazy flakes that would accumulate to inches by nightfall. Another storm coming. Another reason to stay hidden.

I returned to my laptop. The characters still waited, suspended in their conflict.

"What if I can't be who you need me to be?"

I set my fingers on the keys.

Helena stepped back, her heart breaking with each inch of distance. "Then we both already have our answer."

Delete.

Helena reached for him, desperate. "We can figure it out. We can—"

Delete.

Helena lifted her chin, finding strength in the truth. "I need someone who chooses to stay. Every day. Without reservation. Can you do that?"

Jake's silence was answer enough.

I stared at the words. They felt true. They felt final. They felt like dying.

Three days later, my groceries ran out again. No Lily this time—she was giving me space after our conversation. My choices were simple: starve or go to town.

Patterson's General Store was quiet for the day before Thanksgiving. Most people had done their shopping earlier in the week. I grabbed a basket, moving quickly through familiar aisles. Bread, coffee, soup. Nothing that required actual cooking. Nothing that reminded me of sharing meals by firelight.

The parking lot was empty except for two trucks and Mrs. Morrison's sedan. I loaded my bags in the back of my SUV, already calculating how many days before I'd have to do this again.

A forest-green F-250 pulled into the space beside me.

My hands froze on the grocery bag. I knew that truck. Knew the ding in the passenger door, the sound of its engine, the faded firefighter sticker on the back window.

Wyatt cut the engine but didn't get out immediately. Through the windshield, I saw him grip the steering wheel, gathering himself. Then his door opened.

He looked rough. Thinner, shadows under his eyes deep as bruises. His flannel hung loose on his frame. Work boots caked with mud. Three weeks since the storm, but he wore it in every line of his body.

"Emma."

"Wyatt."

We stood there, two parking spaces and a lifetime between us.

"You've been avoiding me." His voice carried no accusation, just fact.

"You've been texting."

"You've been deleting them."

"Seemed easier."

He moved closer, stopping at the hood of my car. "When do you leave?"

The question caught me off guard. "What?"

"For Seattle. Lily didn't say, but I know you. You've got an exit plan. So when?"

My throat tightened. "Four weeks. Right after Christmas."

Something flickered across his face—surprise, hurt, resignation. "I leave for Montana in five weeks."

"I know."

"So that's it? We just... leave?"

"What else is there?"

"We could try—"

"Try what?" The word was a blade. "Long distance? Meeting up between fires? You coming back for holidays you'll probably work through anyway?"

"That's not fair." His jaw went tight, a muscle jumping under his skin.

"Isn't it?" I slammed my trunk harder than necessary. "You're running away, Wyatt. Just like you've done for the last two weeks. Taking every dangerous job, working yourself into the ground rather than deal with what happened between us."

"Running?" He stepped closer, anger flashing in his eyes. "You're the one who won't even read a text message. You're the one hiding in that cabin like a—"

"Like a what?"

"Like a coward."

The word hit like a physical blow. "I'm not the one running. You've been running your whole life."

"At least I'm honest about what I can't give."

"I never asked you to give anything." My voice cracked. "I just asked you to try."

"Try?" He spread his arms wide, exasperated. "Try what? To be someone I'm not? To make promises I can't keep?"

"To stay. To choose something other than leaving. To believe that maybe, just maybe, you're worth staying for."

"And then what?" His voice was barely a whisper, rough with something that sounded like pain. "I fail? Disappoint you? Hurt you worse than I already have? Leave eventually when it gets too hard?"

His questions didn't leave room for a fight. My shoulders slumped, the anger vanishing as if it had never been there, leaving only a hollow ache. "You're leaving now. What's the difference?"

He opened his mouth. Closed it. No answer came.

Snow started falling again, fat flakes that stuck to his hair, his shoulders. He looked lost, standing there in a general store parking lot, unable to give me the one thing I needed—hope that he could change.

"That's what I thought." I pulled my keys from my pocket. "Goodbye, Wyatt."

I got in my car, started the engine. In the rearview mirror, I watched him stand there as I pulled away, getting smaller and smaller until the snow swallowed him whole.

The cabin felt colder when I returned, though the temperature hadn't changed. I set the groceries on the counter, hung up my coat, added wood to the stove. Normal movements in a space that no longer felt normal.

My laptop waited, cursor still blinking.

Jake's silence was answer enough.

I typed the next line.

Helena turned away, knowing that sometimes love wasn't enough. Sometimes two people could want each other desperately and still be wrong. Sometimes the bravest thing was letting go.

The words blurred. I blinked hard, kept typing.

She packed her things with careful precision, each folded shirt a small goodbye. Jake didn't try to stop her. They both knew this was how it had to end—not with screaming or drama, but with the quiet acceptance that some distances were too far to bridge.

Four weeks until Seattle. Five until Montana.

We had our answer.

The Exit Plan

♥

Emma

The boxes watched me from every corner of the cabin.

I'd been packing for three days. Filling them methodically, taping them shut, stacking them by the door. Books in one pile. Kitchen things in another. The few pieces of clothing I'd accumulated since May—thrift store finds, a sweater from the general store, hiking boots broken in on mountain trails I'd never walk again.

Saturday morning. One week until my flight.

I stood at the window with a mug of cold coffee, watching the gray sky threaten snow that wouldn't commit to falling. The mountains looked flat in this light, like a painting someone had left unfinished. No depth. No dimension. Just shapes against shapes.

Behind me, my laptop sat open on the desk. Two documents. Two endings. Neither of them right.

I'd finished the manuscript three days ago. Typed the final period, leaned back in my chair, and waited for the rush of accomplishment that was supposed to come. The celebration. The relief. Two years of work, finally complete.

Nothing came.

The coffee had gone cold hours ago, but I lifted the mug to my lips anyway. Bitter. Stale. I swallowed it like medicine.

My phone showed three missed calls from Jane. I'd let them all go to voicemail. Couldn't face her questions about the ending, about the characters, about whether Helena and Jake found their way back to each other. Couldn't explain that I'd written two versions because I didn't know the answer myself.

A car engine broke the silence. Tires on gravel, that particular crunch I'd learned to recognize over the months. I didn't move from the window.

Her knock was sharp. Impatient.

"It's open."

She pushed through the door, bringing cold air and frustration with her. Her eyes swept the cabin, taking in the boxes, the suitcases, the dismantled life.

"You're really doing this."

"I told you I was leaving."

"Telling and doing are different things." She moved to the kitchen counter, set down a paper bag.

Lily pulled containers from the bag. Soup. Bread. Something that smelled like cinnamon. Her movements were sharp, angry, but I recognized the care beneath them.

"Mason's worried about you."

"Tell him I'm fine."

"He doesn't believe that any more than I do." She turned to face me, arms crossed above her belly. "You're really leaving."

"December 27th. You already knew that."

"I thought you might change your mind."

"Why would I do that?"

"Because you love him."

The words didn't land. They detonated, right in the center of my chest. The coffee in my mug trembled.

"That's exactly why I have to go."

"That makes no sense, Emma."

"It makes perfect sense." I set the mug down harder than I meant to. "Loving him doesn't change who he is. Doesn't change that he'll be in Montana in a few weeks, fighting fires in some wilderness I've never seen. Doesn't change that I'll be here, or in Seattle, or wherever, waiting for him to come back. And then waiting for him to leave again."

"You don't know—"

"Yes, I do." The image hit me—my mother at the kitchen window, her reflection a ghost against the dark glass, waiting. Always waiting. "Every deployment, every single time he walked out that door, she waited. Thirty years of her life spent waiting for a man who was never really there. When he left for good, what did she have left?" I shook my head. "Nothing."

Lily's expression softened. "You're not your mother."

A laugh escaped me, sharp and ugly. "No. I'm worse. My mother stayed. She fought. What do I do? I pack boxes. I book flights. I run."

"Then stop running."

"And do what? Beg him to stay? Watch him panic every time I mention the future?" I pulled Wyatt's flannel tighter around my shoulders—I was still wearing it, had barely taken it off in three weeks. The smell of him was almost gone now, washed away by my own grief. "He looked at me in that parking lot, and I saw it. The same look my father had every time we asked him to choose us over the job. Like staying was a prison sentence."

"Wyatt's not your father."

"No. He's worse." I moved to the window again, pressing my palm against the cold glass. "My father at least pretended he might change. Wyatt won't even try. He told me, Lily. Straight out. He can't be what I need him to be."

"People say things when they're scared."

"And they mean them when they're not."

Lily was quiet for a long moment. I heard her shifting, the soft creak of the floorboards beneath her weight.

"He asks about you."

I closed my eyes. "Don't."

"Every day. What you're doing. If you're eating. If you've left yet."

"Lily—"

"He still hasn't signed the Montana contract."

My hand pressed harder against the glass. "That doesn't mean anything."

"It might."

"It doesn't." I turned to face her. "Two weeks. In two weeks, he'll pack that truck and drive north, same as he's done for years. Me being here won't change that. Me waiting won't change that. The only thing that changes is how much it hurts when he goes."

"So you're leaving first."

"I'm protecting myself."

"You're running."

"Maybe." My throat burned. "But at least I'll be running somewhere instead of standing still, watching him disappear."

Lily shook her head slowly. Her hand moved to her belly again, that protective gesture she'd developed over the past months.

"You know what I think?"

"I'm sure you're going to tell me."

"I think you're terrified. Not of him leaving—you've survived that before. You're terrified he might stay."

The words landed like a physical blow. I felt them settle somewhere beneath my ribs, sharp and uncomfortable.

"That's ridiculous," I said, but my voice came out wrong. Too defensive. Too quick.

"Is it?" Lily moved closer.

No. Stop. I couldn't let this take root. Couldn't let her plant seeds of doubt in the certainty I'd built.

My mind scrambled for purchase, for all the reasons I was right. The evidence. The pattern. The proof.

Wyatt was exactly like my father. The facts lined up perfectly:

Both men who lived for the job, who needed the adrenaline, who couldn't sit still in civilian life. Both men who looked at domesticity like a cage. Both men who said they loved us but chose leaving.

My father's face in the doorway, bag already packed. "I'll be back soon, Em." A lie. He was always leaving. Always choosing the next deployment, the next mission, the next thing that mattered more than we did.

Wyatt in that parking lot. "I can't be what you need me to be." The same resignation. The same inevitability. The same choice, dressed up in different words.

The pattern was clear. Undeniable. I wasn't imagining it.

Except.

A small voice, treacherous and quiet, whispered from somewhere I'd tried to lock away:

What if he's not?

No. I shoved it down, buried it under the weight of thirty years of evidence.

But it persisted, that voice. Insidious. Unwelcome.

What if Wyatt asking "what if I stayed?" wasn't the same as my father's empty promises? What if his panic wasn't about not loving me enough, but about not knowing how to love me right?

What if—

I couldn't. I couldn't let myself go there.

Because if Wyatt wasn't like my father, if this pattern I'd built my entire adult life around was wrong, then everything I'd believed about love, about myself, about what I deserved—all of it would crumble.

And I'd be left standing in the rubble with no one to blame but myself.

The voice whispered again, softer now:

But what if he's not?

The words hit something I hadn't let myself examine. I turned away, busied myself straightening papers on the desk. The manuscript pages. The two endings stacked beside each other.

"That's ridiculous."

"Is it?" Lily moved closer. "If he leaves, you were right all along. Men leave. Love isn't enough. You're better off alone. But if he stays..." She paused. "Then you have to believe you're worth staying for. And you've already decided you're not."

"That's not—"

"Brandon was safe because he was boring. He would have stayed, but you left him. Wyatt was safe because he was leaving. And now that he might not be..." She shrugged. "Now you're the one running."

"You don't know what you're talking about."

"Don't I?" Her voice was soft. "Emma, I've known you for years. The minute it starts to feel permanent, you panic. The cabin getting sold was probably a relief."

"Get out."

"Emma—"

"I mean it." I couldn't look at her. "I can't do this right now. I can't listen to you psychoanalyze my choices when you have no idea—"

"I know you're miserable."

"So is he, apparently. Doesn't mean we should be miserable together."

Lily was quiet. I heard her gather her things, the rustle of her coat.

The door closed softly behind her. I stood frozen in the middle of the cabin, surrounded by boxes and failure.

The laptop screen had gone dark. I touched the trackpad, watched the two documents appear. Two endings. Two futures.

I opened the first one. The happy ending. Helena and Jake on a porch somewhere, older, settled, talking about the years they'd spent together. The compromises they'd made. The love that had survived.

It felt like a lie.

I opened the second one. The sad ending. Helena alone but strong. Jake somewhere else, fighting fires, living his life. Both of them whole, both of them moving on.

It felt true. It also felt like dying.

My phone rang. Jane's number.

I answered without thinking. "Hello."

"Finally." Her voice was sharp, New York fast. "I've been calling for three days."

"Sorry. I've been... busy."

"Too busy to send me a finished manuscript?"

I looked at the two documents on my screen. "It's done."

"And? Is it what we discussed? The big romantic ending?"

My finger hovered over the mouse. "No."

Silence on the line.

"She lets him go," I heard myself say. "He leaves. They both move on. It's realistic."

"Realistic isn't what the publisher asked for."

"It's honest."

"Emma." Jane's voice softened. "Are you okay?"

"I'm fine."

"You don't sound fine."

"The ending is right." I closed the happy version, left only the sad one on the screen. "It's true. People don't change. Some distances can't be bridged. Sometimes the bravest thing is letting go."

"Is this about the book? Or is this about something else?"

I couldn't answer.

"Emma, I've been your agent for three years. I know when you're writing from life." She paused. "The firefighter. The one you mentioned. Is he real?"

"Was real."

"What happened?"

"Nothing. Everything." I pressed my palm against my forehead. "He's leaving. I'm leaving. We decided it was better this way."

"Did you? Or did you decide it for both of you?"

"I have to go."

"Send me the manuscript first."

"I will."

"The real one. Whichever version is true."

She hung up before I could respond.

I stared at the screen. The cursor blinked at the end of the sad ending. Helena, alone but strong. Jake, gone but remembered.

My finger hovered over the 'send' button.

I couldn't press it.

Something was wrong. Not with the writing—the prose was clean, the emotion genuine. The characters felt real. Their pain was earned.

But the ending was a lie.

I minimized the document, opened a blank page. Stared at the white space. Started typing without thinking.

What if I've been asking the wrong question?

The words appeared on the screen, and I felt something shift in my chest.

For five years, I've been asking "will he stay?" Like it's a test. Like love is something he has to prove. But what if that's not the real question?

I kept typing, faster now.

What if the real question is "am I worth staying for?"

And what if I already answered it?

Every time I ran. Every time I packed my bags before he could pack his. Every time I chose to leave instead of risking being left.

I decided I wasn't worth staying for. I decided it before he ever had a chance to choose.

The realization burned through me like wildfire. I pushed back from the desk, the chair scraping against the wooden floor. My father in the doorway, bag in hand. *I'll be back soon.* A lie. He chose the job. He chose leaving. And I chose to believe I wasn't enough to stay for. Brandon was the antidote—safe, present, reliable. He would have stayed. And I left him because staying isn't the same as choosing.

And Wyatt.

I pressed my hands against my eyes. Wyatt, who looked at me like I was sunrise. Wyatt, who ran because staying felt like losing himself. Wyatt, who asked "what if I stayed?" and then panicked when I hoped he meant it.

I'd done the same thing. Panicked. Run. Protected myself from the risk of believing I was worth fighting for.

Lily was right.

I wasn't afraid of him leaving. I was afraid he might stay. Because if he stayed and it still didn't work—if I still wasn't enough—then there was no one left to blame. No patterns to point to. No protection.

Just me, not being enough.

I opened my phone. Scrolled through the deleted messages folder.

Wyatt's texts were still there. Twenty-three of them, spanning three weeks.

Emma, we need to talk about what happened.

I know you're getting these. Please just let me explain.

I'm sorry about what I said. Can we meet?

I don't know how to do this, but I want to try.

I'm still here. I'm not going anywhere.

Please.

I read them all. The desperation. The fear. The hope that kept pushing through despite everything.

He was scared too. Running for different reasons, maybe, but running just the same.

Lily said he hadn't signed the Montana contract. Two weeks until he was supposed to leave, and he still hadn't made it official.

I closed my eyes, imagined him in his apartment above the station. Small space, barely furnished. He'd never bothered to make it a home because he never planned to stay.

The Montana contract would be on his kitchen table. Coffee mug rings staining the corner. He'd pick it up every day, stare at the signature line, put it down again. Why hadn't he decided?

The laptop screen glowed in the dim cabin. Two endings. Two futures.

I couldn't send either one.

The happy ending was a lie because I hadn't earned it yet. Hadn't done the work of believing I was worth staying for. Helena and Jake on that porch, talking about their years together—it rang false because Emma and Wyatt hadn't chosen each other. They'd chosen fear.

The sad ending was a lie too. Helena alone but strong. Jake gone but remembered. It felt true because I'd decided it was—because believing love wasn't enough was easier than risking the alternative.

I closed both documents. Stared at the desktop. A photo of the mountains, taken from the cabin porch on a morning in July when the light had been perfect and the future had felt possible.

One week until my flight. Two weeks until Montana.

Something had to give. I just didn't know what would break first.

The first morning I'd woken up here, the sun had hit the cabin walls just like that. Honey-colored wood and light. I'd stood at the window with my coffee, feeling something I hadn't felt in years.

Home.

Not the cabin itself. The feeling. The possibility.

The snow started falling around midnight. Fat flakes that caught the porch light and swirled like static. I stood at the window in Wyatt's flannel, watching them accumulate on the railing, the steps, the roof of my car.

Another storm coming.

My laptop sat closed on the desk, both endings trapped inside. Unsent. Unfinished. Unresolved.

Lily's words circled through my head like the snow outside.

You're terrified he might stay.

She was right. And she was wrong. And I was too tired to figure out which parts were which.

I pulled the flannel tighter and breathed in deep, searching for any trace of him still left in the fabric.

Nothing.

Just wool and cold and the faint smell of my own grief.

The boxes watched from every corner. The suitcases waited by the door. In seven days, I'd load everything into my car and drive away from the first place that had felt like home in years.

Unless something changed.

Unless I changed.

The thought terrified me more than leaving ever could.

The Search for Tyler

♥

Emma

The coffee in my mug was a cold, bitter memory. I'd been staring at the same blank page on my laptop since noon, hiding in my usual booth at The Copper Cup while the town hummed around me. Outside, December clouds pressed low against the mountains, threatening more snow. Inside, the diner hummed with the clatter of forks and the murmur of Saturday afternoon gossip.

I should have been at the cabin, finishing the manuscript. Should have been packing the last of my boxes. Should have been doing anything other than sitting here, pretending I belonged to a town I was leaving in a few days.

The bell above the door jangled. I didn't look up.

My cursor blinked against white space. Two endings waited in separate files on my desktop, both unsent, both wrong. Helena alone. Helena with Jake. Neither version felt true because I hadn't figured out what true looked like yet.

Static crackled from somewhere behind me.

"—repeat, we have a missing child. Eight years old, male. Last seen on Aspen trail approximately two hours ago. All available units respond."

My fingers froze over the keyboard.

The firefighter at the counter—I recognized him as one of the newer volunteers—was already moving, tossing bills beside his half-eaten pie. His radio squawked again, dispatch coordinates and grid assignments cutting through the diner's warmth.

Eight years old. The Aspen Trail.

I knew those trails. Had hiked every one of them during the long summer months when the cabin felt like sanctuary instead of prison. Knew the terrain, the game paths, the hidden caves where a scared child might shelter.

The diner door crashed open.

Harper Mills stumbled through the door, her face stripped of everything but terror. Her eyes were wide, unfocused, scanning the diner for an answer no one had. She still wore her waitress apron, the Copper Cup logo splashed across the front. Her hair hung loose from its ponytail, and mascara tracked down her cheeks in dark rivers.

"Has anyone seen him?" Her voice cracked, pitched high with panic. "Tyler—my son—he was supposed to wait at the trailhead while I finished my shift. He was right there and then he wasn't and I can't find him, I can't—"

Rita came around the counter, reaching for Harper's shaking hands.

"Honey, slow down. The search teams are already—"

"He's only eight." Harper's knees buckled. "He's only eight and it's getting dark and cold and he doesn't have his inhaler, he left it in my car—"

The door opened again. Cole Rivers stepped through, still in his paramedic jacket. He moved to Harper with the calm efficiency of someone trained for crisis, his hand finding her elbow.

"Harper. Look at me."

She turned, wild-eyed.

"We're going to find him." Cole's voice was steady, certain. "I need you to come with me to the staging area. Can you do that?"

Harper nodded, tears streaming. Cole guided her toward the door, murmuring something too low for me to hear.

I watched them go. Harper's raw maternal terror carved something open in my chest.

My laptop screen glowed. Helena's happy ending. Helena's sad ending. Neither one mattered right now.

A child was lost in the mountains I knew better than anyone who wasn't a local.

I closed my laptop and grabbed my jacket.

Lily intercepted me in the parking lot.

"Emma, stop."

I didn't. My boots crunched across gravel toward my car, keys already in my hand.

"Emma!" She caught my arm, her pregnant belly a curve beneath her winter coat. "What are you doing?"

"A child is missing."

"I know. The search teams are handling it."

"I know those trails." I pulled free, unlocked my door. "I hiked them all summer. The caves, the game paths—"

"It's dangerous. There's a storm system moving through. You're leaving in a week, why would you—"

"Because it's the right thing to do." The words settled the frantic energy in my chest. For the first time in weeks, the path forward wasn't a tangled mess. It was a single, steep trail up a mountain.

"This is about more than Tyler."

"Right now, it's only about Tyler." I slid into the driver's seat. "I'll be careful. I promise."

She stepped back from the car, still watching me. Something shifted in her expression—fear giving way to something that looked almost like hope.

I pulled out of the lot before she could say anything else.

The fire station parking lot had transformed into controlled chaos.

Trucks lined the perimeter, their emergency lights casting red and blue across the gathering dusk. Volunteers clustered around maps spread across truck hoods, their breath forming clouds in the cold air. Floodlights were being erected near the station doors, harsh white circles against the fading afternoon.

I parked at the edge and walked into the chaos.

Mason stood at the center of it, radio in one hand, marker in the other. He was dividing the search area into grids, assigning teams, coordinating with county search and rescue. His voice carried the sharp authority of command.

"—grid four has steep terrain, I want experienced hikers only. Grid seven is dense forest, bring extra lighting—"

He looked up as I approached. Stopped mid-sentence.

"Emma." His jaw tightened. "You should go home. This isn't—"

"I'm an experienced hiker." I held his gaze. "I know that area. I've hiked every trail around there just this summer. I know where a scared kid might hide."

"This is a search and rescue operation. Civilians can't just—"

"Then make me useful." I stepped closer to the maps, pointed at grid five. "There's a cave system here that isn't on any official trail maps. Game path leads to it from the main trail. A child looking for shelter would find it."

Mason studied me. Studied the map. Something in his expression shifted.

"You sure about this?"

"I'm sure."

He opened his mouth—to argue, to dismiss me, I didn't know—but his gaze caught on something over my shoulder. His face went carefully blank.

I turned.

Wyatt stood in the station doorway, fully geared. Technical jacket, hiking boots, pack heavy with emergency equipment. Headlamp strapped to his forehead. Radio clipped to his shoulder.

He stopped dead when he saw me.

The radio chatter, the rumble of an engine, the shouts of volunteers—it all went flat, like sound behind glass. The only thing with any texture was the three weeks of silence stretching between us.

I didn't look away.

He crossed the distance in long strides, his boots heavy on the asphalt.

"What are you doing here?"

No hello. No pretense. Just the question, raw and direct.

"A child is missing." My voice came out steadier than I felt. "I have to help."

His jaw worked. I watched the war play out across his features—surprise, confusion, something that might have been hope.

"You know the terrain?"

"Better than anyone who's not a local."

A long beat. His eyes held mine, searching for something. I didn't know what he found.

"Okay." He turned to Mason. "She's with me."

Mason marked something on his map. "Grid five. The caves Emma mentioned. Radio in every fifteen minutes."

I caught the look that passed between the brothers. Mason's expression said *you're welcome* clear as words.

Wyatt grabbed an extra radio from the equipment table, handed it to me.

"Stay close. Do exactly what I say. If conditions get bad, we turn back. No arguments."

"No arguments."

He studied my face for another moment. Whatever he saw there made something in his shoulders ease.

"Let's go."

Doing It Anyway

Emma

The pines closed in, their branches clutching at the last of the daylight. The world shrank to the narrow, bouncing beam of Wyatt's headlamp and the sound of our boots on wet stone.

Wyatt led, his headlamp cutting a narrow path through the gathering dark. I followed close, my own lamp adding to the weak illumination. The trail climbed steadily, switchbacking up the mountain through dense stands of pine and fir.

Rain had started—light, cold, the kind that seeped through layers and settled in your bones. The cold started to bite, a damp chill that sank through my jacket and settled in my bones. My breath formed clouds that the wind immediately shredded.

We didn't talk.

There was nothing to say that mattered more than finding Tyler. Nothing that couldn't wait until a child was safe and warm and breathing.

Wyatt moved with the easy confidence of someone who belonged in these mountains. His stride was efficient, his breathing measured.

Every few minutes he'd pause, scanning the tree line, calling Tyler's name into the darkness.

He didn't hesitate. Didn't question. When the call came in about a missing child, he'd simply moved—grabbing gear, coordinating teams, his voice steady on the radio even as everyone else's cracked with panic.

I'd spent three weeks calling him a coward. Telling myself he ran from everything that mattered.

But watching him now—the way he read the mountain, the way he moved with purpose through terrain that would break most people—I saw something different.

This was who he was. Someone who ran toward danger, not away from it. Someone who chose, every single time, to put himself between harm and the people who needed protecting.

What if I'd been wrong? What if the bravest person I knew was the one I'd been pushing away?

I watched the slope below us, the brush, the shadows between tree trunks. Looking for any sign of a scared eight-year-old trying to find his way home.

"Trail splits ahead." Wyatt's voice cut through the wind. "Main path goes left. Where's this game path you mentioned?"

I moved past him, found the gap in the brush I remembered from summer. Marked by a lightning-scarred pine, barely visible in the dark.

"Here."

He nodded, let me lead.

The game path was narrow, treacherous. Animal trails carved into the mountainside, all loose rock and exposed roots. My boots slipped twice; Wyatt's hand caught my elbow both times without comment.

We called Tyler's name into the darkness. Only the wind answered.

Twenty minutes in, I saw it.

A flash of red against brown brush. Wrong color for the forest, too bright, too clean.

"Wyatt."

He was beside me in two strides. I pointed.

Tyler's backpack hung from a broken branch, its Spider-Man design soaked dark with rain. One strap had torn loose. The main compartment gaped open, a single granola bar spilling out.

"He was here." Wyatt crouched, examined the ground. "Tracks lead that direction. Fresh."

"The caves are a quarter mile up this ridge."

He looked at me. In the harsh light of our headlamps, his face was all shadows and sharp angles.

"You didn't have to come out here," he said quietly.

"Yes, I did."

Something shifted in his expression. Recognition, maybe. Or respect.

"Lead the way."

We found him in the third cave.

Near the caves I'd found behind the waterfall. Not really a cave—more of an overhang, a depression in the rock face where some ancient force had carved shelter from the wind. The opening was narrow, barely three feet high. I had to crouch to look inside.

Tyler huddled in the far corner, knees pulled to his chest, arms wrapped around his shins. His lips were blue. His skin was gray. He was shivering so hard I could hear his teeth chattering from six feet away.

"Tyler." I kept my voice soft. "Tyler, can you hear me?"

His head lifted. Eyes too big in his pale face, pupils blown wide with cold and fear.

"I'm Emma. I'm here to help. Can I come in?"

A tiny nod.

I crawled into the cave, the rock scraping my back. Behind me, Wyatt was already pulling thermal blankets from his pack, relaying our coordinates into his radio.

"Grid five, we have the child. Repeat, we have the child. Hypothermic, conscious and responsive. Need immediate evac."

I reached Tyler, knelt in front of him. His whole body trembled.

"Hey, buddy." I stripped off my gloves, pressed my warm hands to his frozen cheeks. "Your mom is waiting for you. She's so worried. We're going to get you back to her, okay?"

"I got lost." His voice was thin, reedy. "The path looked the same and then it wasn't and I couldn't find my way back and it got dark and I was scared—"

"I know. I know you were scared." I rubbed his arms through his soaked jacket, trying to generate any warmth. "You were so smart to find shelter. So smart to stay put."

Wyatt crawled in beside us, the space suddenly cramped and small. He moved with practiced efficiency—thermal blanket wrapped around Tyler's shoulders, hands checking pulse, flashlight in Tyler's eyes to check pupil response.

"Tyler, I need you to drink this." He produced a small thermos from his pack. "It's warm. It'll help."

Tyler's hands shook too badly to hold it. I steadied the thermos while Wyatt guided it to the boy's lips.

"Small sips. That's it. Good job."

The radio crackled. Mason's voice: "Copy grid five. Helicopter is twenty minutes out. Can you get him to the meadow at the trailhead?"

Wyatt looked at Tyler's trembling form, at the steep terrain outside. "Negative. We'll need a litter team. Send coordinates for ground extraction."

"Copy. Litter team en route. Hold your position."

Tyler's hand found mine, his fingers ice-cold even through the thermal blanket.

"Am I going to be okay?"

"You're going to be just fine." I squeezed his hand gently. "We found you. The hard part is over."

"I was really scared."

The words came out small, shameful. Like admitting fear was something to be ashamed of.

I brushed wet hair back from his forehead. The words that came out weren't mine; they were a ghost's. "My dad used to say that. Before every deployment." I swallowed against the sudden burn in my throat. "Being scared is okay. Being brave means doing it anyway."

The cave went quiet enough to hear the rain dripping from the rock outside. I didn't have to look to know Wyatt was staring at me. The weight of his gaze was a physical thing.

"You stayed in the cave even though you were scared," I continued, my voice steady. "You didn't panic, didn't keep running. That's brave, Tyler. That's the bravest thing there is."

Tyler's grip on my hand tightened. A small nod.

"My mom's going to be mad."

"Your mom is going to be so happy to see you she won't have room to be mad." I smiled at him. "Trust me."

Wyatt shifted beside us, adjusting the thermal blanket higher around Tyler's chin. His hands were steady, competent. He'd checked Tyler's vitals three times in the last ten minutes, his touch gentle but thorough. Professional. Caring.

He could have stayed at the staging area. Could have coordinated from there, let the field teams do the searching. But he hadn't. He'd grabbed his pack and headed into the mountains without a second thought.

For a child he didn't know. For a family that wasn't his.

Because that's what he did. That's who he was.

This was who he was—the person who walked into danger so others could walk out. Who chose, every single day, to put himself between someone else and harm.

Not because it was easy. Because it was right.

"Litter team is ten minutes out." Wyatt's voice was quiet. "How are you feeling, buddy? Any warmer?"

Tyler nodded. Color was returning to his cheeks, faint pink beneath the cold-pale. His shivering had eased from violent tremors to occasional shivers.

"I want my mom."

"She's waiting for you." Wyatt's hand rested briefly on Tyler's shoulder. "You'll see her soon."

We settled into waiting. The cave was too small, too close. Every breath I took filled with the smell of wet stone and fear-sweat and Wyatt—pine and cold and something underneath that was just him.

I kept my attention on Tyler. Kept talking to him in low, soothing tones about nothing important. Asked about his favorite superhero (Spider-Man, obviously). About school. About what he wanted for Christmas.

But I felt Wyatt watching.

Not Tyler. Me.

Every time I shifted, I caught his eyes on my face. Every time I smiled at Tyler, I saw something flicker in his expression.

When Tyler's eyes drifted closed—not unconscious, just exhausted—Wyatt finally spoke.

"You didn't have to come."

I looked at him. In the harsh light, his face was raw, unguarded. The mask he'd worn for three weeks was gone.

"Yes. I did."

"Emma—"

"Not now." I glanced at Tyler, sleeping restlessly against the emergency blanket. "He needs us focused."

Wyatt's jaw tightened. He nodded.

But his hand found mine in the darkness. Just for a moment. Just long enough for his fingers to press against my palm, warm and solid and real.

I didn't pull away.

Wyatt

She'd come.

That was the thought that kept circling through my mind as we waited for the litter team. Emma had come. Into the mountains, in the dark, in dangerous terrain—she'd come without hesitation.

I watched her with Tyler. The way she kept him talking, kept him focused. The gentle pressure of her hands as she rubbed warmth back into his arms. The soft reassurance in her voice.

Competent. Compassionate. Completely present.

This was who she was. Not someone who ran when things got hard. Not someone who gave up.

A fighter. Someone who fought for what mattered.

And I'd been letting her go.

For three weeks, I'd been telling myself it was better this way. Cleaner. Safer for both of us. I'd convinced myself that walking away was the right thing to do.

But watching her now—seeing her strength, her steadiness, the way she showed up even when it was hard—I saw the truth I'd been avoiding.

She wasn't the one who ran.

I was.

And I'd been calling it protection. Calling it sacrifice. Calling it anything but what it really was: fear.

"Tyler's going to be okay," Emma said softly, her eyes still on the boy. "Because of you. You got us here in time."

"We got him here," I corrected. "You knew where to look."

She glanced at me then, and in the dim light of the cave, I saw everything I'd been too afraid to acknowledge. Everything I'd been running from.

Everything I was done running from.

"Emma—"

"Not now." Her voice was gentle but firm. "He needs us focused."

She was right. Tyler came first. Everything else could wait.

But when the litter team arrived, when this was over—

We were going to talk.

And this time, I wasn't going to run.

Emma

The litter team arrived in a chaos of voices and equipment.

Four firefighters I half-recognized from trips to town, their faces taut with professional focus. They secured Tyler to the stretcher with practiced ease, checking vitals, adjusting blankets, moving with the kind of seamless coordination that came from training and trust.

Wyatt and I followed them down the mountain.

The terrain was treacherous in the dark—loose rock, slick mud, branches whipping across the trail. The team moved carefully, mindful of their precious cargo. Tyler's mother's name echoed through the radio chatter like a prayer. *Harper. We're bringing him to Harper.*

By the time we reached the staging area, a crowd had gathered.

Harper Mills stood at the edge of the parking lot, Cole Rivers's hand on her shoulder. When she saw the litter emerge from the tree line, she broke into a run.

"Tyler! Tyler, baby—"

The medical team intercepted her gently, explained about hypothermia, about hospital transport, about the next few hours. Harper barely heard them. Her entire being was focused on her son's pale face, his small hand reaching for hers.

"Mommy."

Harper sobbed, pressing her forehead to Tyler's. "I'm here, baby. I'm right here. I'm never letting you go."

The helicopter's rotors beat the air as it descended into the meadow. Lights, noise, organized chaos. Tyler was loaded aboard with Harper beside him, Cole climbing in to monitor vitals during transport.

And then they were gone.

The helicopter's rotors faded, leaving a ringing silence broken only by the wind and the soft sobs of the remaining volunteers.

Wyatt stood beside me, both of us splattered with mud, soaked through, exhausted. The adrenaline was fading, leaving something raw and exposed in its wake.

I became aware of the crowd watching us. Lily near the station door, her hand pressed to her mouth. Mason with his radio silent for the first time in hours. The crew, the volunteers, the town.

All of them looking at us. At me and Wyatt, standing close enough to touch.

"We need to talk."

Wyatt's voice was low, meant only for me.

I turned to face him.

His eyes held mine. Gray and steady. Terrified. Hopeful. He didn't have to say a word; I could see my own reflection in the storm raging there.

"We need to talk," he repeated. Not a question. Not a request.

A commitment.

The wind cut between us, sharp with coming snow. My body ached from the climb, the cold, the hours of searching. My heart ached from something else entirely.

I nodded.

Scared.

Hopeful.

Ready.

Staying WITH You

♥

Emma

The hospital's fluorescent lights hit me like an accusation.

After hours in the dark—the wet pine, the narrow beam of headlamps, Tyler's small body shaking against mine—this brightness felt like violence. I blinked against it, my eyes watering. The emergency department smelled like antiseptic and floor polish and something underneath that was pure fear. Or maybe that was just me.

Wyatt's hand found the small of my back as we pushed through the automatic doors. The contact burned through my damp jacket. I should have stepped away. Should have created distance. Instead I leaned into it, just for a second, letting his warmth anchor me to the present.

Mason and Lily stood in the waiting area, two familiar shapes against the institutional beige walls. Lily saw us first. She crossed the room in three strides and pulled me into a hug that smelled like coffee and wool and home.

"He's okay." Her voice was thick. "Tyler's okay. They're treating him for hypothermia but he's going to be fine."

The words washed the last of the strength from my bones. My knees buckled and I sagged against her, the adrenaline I'd been running on for hours finally gone. We'd found him. He was alive. The rest of it—the cave, the cold, Wyatt's hand in mine—could wait.

"Harper?" My voice came out rough.

"With him. Won't leave his side." Lily pulled back, studied my face. Her eyes were too knowing. "You look like hell."

"Feel like it."

Mason appeared at Wyatt's shoulder. Mason met Wyatt's gaze over my shoulder. Mason gave a short, sharp nod, his jaw relaxing for the first time all night. A silent message passed between them—*you were right to bring her.*

"Cole's been with Tyler since they landed." Mason's voice was calm, professional. Chief Drake giving a report. "Body temperature rising. No signs of frostbite. Lungs are clear."

The curtain at the far end of the treatment area rustled. Cole Rivers emerged, still in his paramedic uniform, stethoscope draped around his neck. Exhaustion carved lines around his eyes, but his expression held something softer than fatigue. Something like tenderness.

"He's asking for juice." Cole's mouth quirked. "Pretty sure that's a good sign."

From behind the curtain, Tyler's voice: "Uncle Cole? Can I have apple? The red kind?"

Uncle Cole.

I watched Cole's face transform. The professional mask slipped, replaced by something raw and unguarded. He glanced toward the curtain, then back at us, something like apology in his expression.

"He's my—" Cole stopped, glancing at Harper. "My brother... is Harper's ex-husband." The words were clipped, an explanation offered to the room but meant for someone else entirely.

Before any of us could respond, Harper appeared in the doorway. Her hair was wild, her face streaked with dried tears, her hands clutching Tyler's jacket like she'd never let go of anything again. But she was smiling. Really smiling.

"Thank you." Her voice cracked on the words. "All of you. I can't—you saved my son. You saved—"

She broke off, pressing her hand to her mouth. Cole moved toward her, stopped himself, took a step back. The space between them hummed with something complicated and old.

I watched the scene unfold—Harper's overwhelming gratitude, Cole's careful distance, Mason coordinating with the hospital staff, Lily making sure everyone had coffee.

I looked down at my own boots, caked with mud and forest debris, leaving a dirty puddle on the polished linoleum. I was a mess tracked in from the outside. A temporary problem that had been solved, now standing on the periphery of a life I had no claim to.

This was where I always ended up. On the periphery. Close enough to see what I couldn't have.

I took a step toward the exit. Then another. No one would notice if I slipped away. I could call a cab, get back to my car at the staging area, drive to the cabin, pack what was left—

"Don't."

Wyatt's hand closed around my wrist. His grip was warm, solid, unrelenting.

"Please."

I turned to face him. In the harsh fluorescent light, he looked half-wild. Mud caked his boots and climbed his pants. His jacket was torn at one shoulder. Dark stubble shadowed his jaw, and exhaustion hollowed the skin beneath his eyes. But those eyes—gray as storm clouds, fixed on mine with an intensity that made my breath catch.

"Wyatt, I can't do this again—"

"I turned down Montana."

The words didn't make sense. I heard them—the syllables, the sounds—but my brain refused to process their meaning.

"What?"

"Called them yesterday evening." He released my wrist but didn't step back. "Took a permanent position with Copper Ridge Fire Department."

The floor tilted. The fluorescent buzz grew deafening. I gripped the back of a plastic chair to stay upright.

"You—" I couldn't finish the sentence.

"I'm staying." His voice dropped low. "Here. In Copper Ridge. Permanently."

I looked past him to Mason, who stood with his arm around Lily. His expression said he already knew what Wyatt was telling me.

"When?" The word scraped out of me.

"Made the decision two days ago. Called Mac this afternoon to make it official." Wyatt's jaw tightened. "Should have told you sooner. Should have told you a lot of things sooner. But truthfully, you were making it hard to talk to you."

The hospital sounds faded—the beeping monitors, the hushed conversations, the squeak of rubber soles on linoleum. All I could hear was my own pulse hammering in my ears.

"We need to talk." Wyatt's hand found mine. "Outside. Now."

The December air hit like a slap. After the hospital's artificial warmth, the cold was a shock—sharp, clean, real. Snow fell in soft curtains, catching the light from the parking lot lamps. My breath formed clouds that the wind immediately scattered.

Wyatt led me away from the emergency entrance, toward the far edge of the lot where his truck sat alone under a flickering streetlight. We stopped beside the tailgate, snow accumulating on its surface.

I wrapped my arms around myself. Not just against the cold. Against the hope.

"Why?" The word came out broken. "Why would you do that? Montana was your dream—"

"No." He turned to face me, and the raw vulnerability in his expression stole my next breath. "Montana was my escape. There's a difference."

"Wyatt—"

"I've been an idiot." The confession came fast, the words tumbling over each other. "A complete, stubborn, terrified idiot. For five years, I've been running. From this. From what happened in Portland. Every time you walk into a room, Emma, I have to fight the urge to either run for the hills or pin you to the nearest wall. There's no in-between."

My throat closed. I couldn't speak. Could barely breathe.

"I thought commitment meant losing myself." He dragged a hand through his hair, leaving it standing in damp spikes. "Watched Mason give up everything when Dad died. His future. His freedom. His entire life to raise me and James. And I swore I'd never do that. Never let myself get trapped."

"Mason didn't—"

"I know." He swallowed, his throat working. "I see that now. He wasn't trapped. He was choosing. Choosing what mattered. And he got everything he ever wanted because of it."

Snow caught in his eyelashes. Melted on his cheeks like tears.

"You matter, Emma." He stepped closer, close enough that I could feel his body heat cutting through the cold. "You're what matters. The only thing that's mattered in years."

"You don't have to stay for me." The words hurt coming out. "I never asked you to change your life. To give up—"

"I'm not staying for you." He cupped my face in his hands, his palms warm against my frozen cheeks. "I'm staying *with* you. There's a difference."

The words hit me like a physical blow. I'm staying with you.

Two manuscript endings flashed through my mind. The happy one—Wyatt sweeping me off my feet, declaring his love, everything falling into place like a fairy tale. The sad one—me walking away noble and wounded, protecting myself from the inevitable hurt.

Both were lies.

The happy ending was a fantasy I'd written to avoid the terrifying reality that love doesn't solve everything. That choosing someone means choosing them again tomorrow, and the day after that, in a thousand small unglamorous moments. The sad ending was armor. A defense mechanism. If I wrote the tragedy myself, at least I'd be in control of the pain.

But this—standing in a snowy parking lot, both of us exhausted and muddy and scared—this was the truth. Messy. Terrifying. Not a destiny I could write for myself. A choice I had to make right now, in this moment, with no guarantee of how the story would end.

I'd been trying to write our ending before we'd even begun. Trying to control the narrative so I wouldn't get hurt. But that wasn't bravery. That was just another form of running.

The distinction hit me like a punch to the chest. Not sacrifice. Not obligation. Choice.

"You're the bravest person I know." His thumbs traced my cheekbones, wiping away tears I hadn't realized I'd shed. "You left your safe life in Seattle. Broke off an engagement because you knew it was wrong. Came to this tiny mountain town to write your truth. And tonight—God, Emma—you showed up when it mattered. Walked into that forest to find a kid you'd never met."

"I was scared."

"I know." His forehead pressed against mine. "Being scared is okay. Being brave means doing it anyway. Sound familiar?"

My father's words. The ones I'd whispered to Tyler in that cave. The ones Wyatt had heard and remembered.

"I'm terrified you'll change your mind." The admission scraped out of me, raw and honest. "That you'll wake up in six months and realize you made a mistake. That you'll resent me for keeping you here."

"Then watch me prove you wrong." His voice dropped to something rough and certain. "Every single day. For the rest of my life if you let me."

"Okay." The word came out before I could overthink it. Before I could retreat into my head and write a safer ending. This wasn't capitulation. This wasn't me giving in to the fantasy. This was me choosing—consciously, deliberately—to step into the unknown. "Yes, I want to be here with you."

I launched myself at him.

There was no other word for it. One second I was standing there, shaking with cold and fear and hope. The next my arms were around his neck and my body was pressed against his and my mouth was on his mouth.

He caught me. Lifted me off my feet. His mouth was cold from the snow and tasted of coffee and desperation. It wasn't a gentle kiss. It was a collision. His hands gripped my waist, bruising, pulling me tight against him until I couldn't tell where the cold ended and his heat began.

"I love you." The words spilled out between kisses. "I love you. I think I've loved you for five years."

"I know." His voice was rough against my lips. "I know. I'm sorry it took me so long to catch up."

He broke the kiss only to claim my mouth again, slower this time, a deep, thorough kiss that spoke of forevers, not just tonight.

When we finally broke apart, I was laughing. Or crying. Possibly both. My face was wet with melted snow and tears, and I didn't care.

"I don't even have anywhere to live." The practical concern surfaced through the joy. "The cabin sold. Dorothy needs possession by January. I was going back to Seattle—"

"About that." Wyatt's expression shifted. Something nervous flickered across his features. Almost shy.

"What?"

"I called Aunt Dorothy three weeks ago."

My heart stopped.

"Made her an offer on the cabin."

"You what?"

"I saw you in that cabin during the storm." His hands tightened on my waist. "The way you fit in those rooms. You belonged there, Emma. I couldn't stand the thought of anyone else living in your home."

"Wyatt, you can't afford—" The protest died in my throat as I registered what he was saying.

"Mason co-signed the loan. And Dorothy gave me a family discount—said she'd rather see it go to someone who'd love it than some developer from California." His voice gained strength, certainty. "I used my hazard pay savings. Five years of smokejumping, Emma. Money I never spent because I never had a home to put it into. Never had a reason to stop running."

His hands framed my face, forcing me to hold his gaze. "The cabin isn't just for you. It's my anchor. My reason to finally stay in one place. I'm not giving up Montana for you—I'm choosing this. Choosing us. Choosing to stop running from the only thing that's ever felt like home."

He reached into his jacket pocket, pulled out a crumpled piece of paper. My handwriting stared back at me. The discarded ending. The sad one.

"Found this in your cabin when I was looking for things to burn during the storm, and I couldn't stop thinking about it. That's when the idea hit me." His voice went rough. "You were writing our ending before we even had a beginning. Writing yourself heartbreak like it was inevitable."

My breath caught.

"I bought the cabin so we can have a happy ending." He pressed the paper into my palm, closed my fingers around it. "I'm showing you that I am staying, and I want it to be us in that cabin. Whatever comes next—we choose it. Together."

He swallowed hard. "It's ours. If you want it to be."

Ours.

The word hung between us, heavy with meaning. Not his. Not mine. Ours.

"The cabin." I couldn't make my voice work properly. "You bought the cabin."

I kissed him. Hard. Desperate. My hands fisted in his jacket, pulling him closer, trying to pour every feeling I couldn't articulate into that single point of contact.

"Yes." I breathed the word against his mouth. "Yes. A thousand times yes."

His laugh vibrated through both of us. He lifted me again, spun me once, and the snow swirled around us like a blessing.

When he set me down, I was crying in earnest. Big, messy sobs that should have been embarrassing but somehow weren't. Because he was crying too. Wyatt Drake, smokejumper, man who ran from everything, standing in a hospital parking lot with tears on his cheeks and snow in his hair and a future in his hands.

"I love you." He pressed his forehead to mine. "I should have said it sooner. Should have chased you down when you left and told you—"

"You're saying it now." I pressed my palm to his chest, feeling his heart pound beneath the layers of wet fleece. "That's what matters."

"Our cabin." He tested the words. Smiled at them. "Our home."

"Our home."

The snow kept falling. Soft, steady, accumulating on his shoulders and in my hair. The cold should have been unbearable—we were both soaked, both exhausted, both running on nothing but adrenaline and love. But I was warm. Warmer than I'd been in five years.

Wyatt pulled me against his chest, tucking my head under his chin. I listened to his heartbeat, felt his breath stir my hair. The mountains rose dark against the lighter sky, and somewhere in those peaks, a cabin waited for us. A cabin that was no longer an escape. A place that was no longer temporary.

Home.

Not a location. A choice.

I'd spent so long running from the risk of loss that I'd forgotten what it felt like to gain something worth keeping. Standing in that parking lot, wrapped in Wyatt's arms, I remembered.

"We should go inside." His voice rumbled through his chest. "Let them know we're okay."

"In a minute."

"You're freezing."

"Don't care."

His arms tightened around me. "Neither do I."

The snow fell. The world held still.

Epilogue: Drip and Rot

♥

Emma

Two weeks later, the dirt road to the Ponderosa Cabin looked different.

Not because of the snow—though there was plenty of that, three feet of pristine white blanketing everything from the pines to the peaks. Not because of the winter light, crystalline and sharp, turning each icicle into a prism.

His hand found mine across the center console, calloused fingers threading through my own like they belonged there. The silence in the cab wasn't empty like it used to be between us; it was full. A shared breath. The knowledge that this time, at the end of this road, neither of us was leaving.

"You're quiet." His voice was soft, no pressure in it.

"Just thinking."

"Dangerous habit."

I laughed, the sound startling in the truck's warm cab. "Says the man who jumped out of airplanes into forest fires."

"That's not thinking. That's reacting." His thumb traced circles on my palm. "Thinking is what you do. The spiral thing."

"I'm not spiraling."

"No?"

"No." I turned to look at him—sun catching the lighter streaks in his brown hair, gray eyes focused on the road ahead, the determined set of his jaw. "I'm just... taking it in."

Then it was there, tucked into the pines. Cedar siding dark against the white, a heavy blanket of snow on its green metal roof, icicles hanging from the eaves like crystal teeth. Smoke didn't rise from the chimney yet, but it would. Soon.

Wyatt killed the engine. Neither of us moved.

"I cleared the deck yesterday." His voice was rough. "Wanted it to be ready."

"You came up here without me?"

"Had to make sure the pipes didn't freeze."

I understood that. The past two weeks had felt like a dream I kept expecting to wake from—the hospital parking lot, the snow falling around us, his confession that he'd bought this cabin. Our cabin. The words still didn't quite fit in my mouth.

Wyatt reached into his jacket pocket and pulled out a set of keys. He pressed them into my palm. The metal was warm from his body, heavy. Two simple brass keys on a steel ring. I stared at them, my throat closing. Not a rental key to be returned. Not a temporary pass. A key to a door I would lock from the inside, with him.

"I can't believe you did this." My voice cracked on the last word.

"I was terrified you'd think it was too much. Too fast." He swallowed. "That maybe I'd pushed too hard, and you'd—"

"It is too much." I looked up, found his eyes. "And too fast. And absolutely perfect."

His shoulders, which I hadn't realized were tight, dropped. The long breath he let out fogged the air between us, taking the last of his tension with it.

"Let's go inside."

The front door swung open on hinges that needed oil. I made a mental note—the first of many, I suspected. The cold hit immediately, sharp and clean, but beneath it lingered something familiar. Cedar. Old books. The faint ghost of woodsmoke from fires past.

Home.

"Generator's new." Wyatt moved past me toward the wood stove. "Had it installed last week. Won't fail this time."

"That's reassuring." I watched him crouch by the stove, his movements efficient and sure. "Given that the old one almost killed us."

"Technically, the storm almost killed us." He struck a match, held it to the kindling. "The generator just made things interesting."

"That's one word for it."

Flame caught. Spread. The first crackle of burning wood filled the silence.

I walked deeper into the cabin, running my fingers along surfaces I'd touched a hundred times before. The back of the couch. The edge of the kitchen counter. The windowsill where I'd watched the storm rage, certain I was going to freeze to death in a cabin that wasn't mine.

But it was mine now. Ours.

"What are you thinking?" Wyatt appeared behind me, close enough that I felt his warmth.

"That I used to stand here and pretend." I pressed my palm flat against the cold glass. "Pretend this was my life. My view. My home.

Then I'd remember it was temporary, and I'd pack my heart back up before it could get too attached."

"And now?"

"Now I don't have to pretend."

His arms came around me from behind, pulling me back against his chest. We stood there, looking out at the mountains—white peaks against blue sky, endless and eternal, a view that had witnessed a hundred years of lives and would witness a hundred more.

"Fair warning," he said, his voice taking on a different tone. Not apologetic, exactly. Matter-of-fact. "I made a list this morning."

"A list?"

"Of everything that needs fixing." He pulled back slightly, and I turned to face him. His expression was serious now, the romantic moment giving way to practical reality. "The roof needs work—there's damage on the south side I didn't catch until yesterday. Snow load's been hard on it."

I glanced up reflexively, as if I could see through the ceiling to the problem above.

"The deck boards are rotting," he continued. "Northeast corner, mostly, but I found soft spots near the steps too. Whole thing probably needs to be rebuilt in the next year or two."

"Okay." I tried to keep my voice steady, but something in my chest tightened. Not panic. Just... reality, settling in with weight.

"Kitchen faucet drips. I tried tightening it, but the washer's shot. Probably need to replace the whole fixture." He was ticking items off mentally, his gaze moving around the cabin. "Bedroom window sticks—frame's warped from moisture. And I'm pretty sure there's something living in the walls. Squirrels, maybe. Or mice."

The list kept coming. Insulation that needed upgrading. Floorboards that creaked and sagged. A chimney that should be inspected before we relied on it too heavily. Electrical outlets that sparked. A bathroom door that wouldn't latch properly.

"The porch railing's loose," he added. "And there's rot in the window trim on the west side. Water damage, looks like. Might go deeper than what I can see."

I stared at him. "Is that all?"

"For now." A ghost of a smile touched his lips. "I'm sure we'll find more once we really start living here."

The weight of it settled over me—not crushing, but present. Real. This wasn't the fantasy cabin from my rental days, where problems were someone else's responsibility. This was ours. Every drip, every creak, every rotting board.

"Sounds expensive," I said finally.

"Probably." His arms tightened around me. "And time-consuming. And frustrating. Some of this stuff, I can fix myself. Some of it..." He shook his head. "We'll need help. Professional help."

"So it's a disaster."

"It's a project." His voice was firm. "There's a difference."

I looked around the cabin again, seeing it differently now. Not through the rose-colored lens of romance, but through the harsh light of reality. The water stain on the ceiling. The gap under the front door where cold air whistled through. The way the floor sloped slightly toward the kitchen, probably from settling.

It wasn't perfect. It wasn't even close to perfect.

And somehow, that made it more real. More ours.

"It's not a fairy-tale castle," I said softly.

"No." Wyatt's breath stirred my hair. "It's better. It's real. And we'll build it together. Fix what's broken. Strengthen what's weak. Make it what we need it to be."

Build together. The words resonated in my chest, settling into place like the final piece of a puzzle I'd been working on for five years.

"I spent so long looking for perfect," I said. "Perfect career. Perfect relationship. Perfect life. And it was all just... pretend. Pretty words on a page that didn't mean anything."

"And now?"

"Now I want real." I turned in his arms again, meeting his eyes. "Even if real means rotting deck boards and dripping faucets and things living in the walls."

"Especially if it means that." His smile was crooked, genuine. "Because that's what life actually looks like. Not the Instagram version. The real version."

"The version where we fix things as they break."

"And break things as we fix them, probably." He laughed. "I'm not exactly a master carpenter."

"We'll learn." The certainty in my voice surprised me. "Together."

He kissed my forehead, and I felt the gesture all the way through me. Not passionate, not desperate—just steady. Solid. Real.

"First project," he said. "That faucet. It's been driving me crazy for two days."

"First project," I agreed. "Then the window. Then the deck. Then—"

"Then everything else." He pulled back, his hands framing my face. "One thing at a time. No rush. We've got the rest of our lives."

The rest of our lives. In a cabin that leaked and creaked and needed more work than either of us probably understood yet. In a life that wouldn't be perfect, wouldn't be easy, wouldn't look anything like the stories I used to write.

But it would be ours. Built together, one repair at a time.

"Show me the worst of it," I said. "I want to see what we're up against."

Wyatt's eyebrows rose. "Now?"

"Now. No more pretending. No more fantasy. Show me the real thing."

So he did.

Wyatt

The fire station smelled like coffee and chili and something sugary—Luke's girlfriend had dropped off cookies, apparently, and the crew had demolished half of them before Emma and I walked through the door.

"There they are!" Javi stood from the long table, arms spread wide. "The lovebirds emerge from their nest."

"We weren't hiding." Emma's cheeks flushed pink. "We were unpacking."

"Is that what they call it now?"

I punched his shoulder as I passed. "Shut up, Martinez."

The day room was crowded—everyone had turned out for team lunch, a tradition Mason had started years ago that had somehow survived every schedule change and staffing shuffle. My brother sat at the head of the table, Lily tucked against his side, her hand resting on his forearm like she couldn't stop touching him.

James and Madison had claimed the corner, Madison's belly round beneath her sweater. Six months along, and she glowed with it—that particular kind of radiance pregnant women got, like they were lit from within.

"Hey." James caught my eye, nodded. A whole conversation in that single gesture: *you good? she good? everything good?*

I nodded back. *All good.*

Emma had been pulled into conversation with Lily, their heads bent together, voices low. I watched them—two women who'd found their way into this family through sheer stubborn persistence. Through choosing us even when we made it difficult.

"Attention, everyone." Mason stood, and the room quieted. My brother didn't have to raise his voice to command a space. Never had. "Before we eat, I have an announcement."

Lily's face split into a grin. She couldn't contain it, whatever secret they were holding.

"Lily and I—" Mason's voice caught. He cleared his throat, tried again. "We're expecting. Baby's due in July."

The room erupted. Cheers, applause, someone—probably Luke—letting out a whoop that rattled the windows. I was on my feet before I knew I'd moved, pulling my brother into a hug that probably crushed a few ribs.

"Congratulations." The word felt inadequate. "Mason, that's—"

"I know." His voice was rough against my shoulder. "I know."

When I released him, Lily was there, and I hugged her too—carefully, like the baby might break if I squeezed too hard.

"July," she said. "Same month as the anniversary of when we met."

"Fitting." I grinned at her. "You'll always remember how much you hated him at first."

"I didn't hate him. I found him obstinate and unreasonable."

"That's called hate, Inspector."

She laughed, and the sound was so different from the guarded woman who'd walked into this station eight months ago. Lighter. Freer.

Emma appeared at my elbow, her hand finding mine. "July babies are supposed to be lucky."

"Are they?"

"I read it somewhere." Her smile was soft. "Probably made it up."

Emma

The celebration was in full swing when my phone rang. A baby. A family growing. My heart felt full to bursting for them, a sweet ache for a future I was just starting to let myself imagine.

I almost ignored the call—the noise, the warmth, the family surrounding me felt too precious to interrupt. But the screen showed Jane Harper's name, and my agent didn't call for small talk.

"Sorry." I held up the phone. "I have to—"

"Go." Wyatt squeezed my hand. "I'll save you some cookies."

I ducked into the hallway, pressed the phone to my ear. "Jane?"

"Emma." Her voice was crisp, professional, but something underneath it vibrated with energy. "I just got off a call with Horizon Books."

My heart stopped. Started again. "And?"

"They want it. The full manuscript. They're offering five figures."

Six figures. The number echoed in the hallway, a foreign sound. I pressed my back against the wall, my knees suddenly weak. It wasn't about the money. It was the validation. The proof that leaving Seattle, coming here, breaking my own heart and putting it back together on the page—it had all meant something.

"Emma? Are you there?"

"I'm here." My voice sounded far away.

"Low five, but yes. With options for the next two books if this one performs." A pause. "You did it. The ending—whatever you changed in those final chapters—it worked. They said it was the most authentic romance they'd read in years."

Authentic. Because I'd lived it. Because I'd stopped writing what I thought love should look like and started writing what it actually felt like.

Because I'd written about the dripping faucets and rotting deck boards alongside the grand gestures. Because I'd made my characters build something real instead of just falling into something perfect.

"Emma?"

"I'm here." I pressed my back against the hallway wall. "I just—I need a minute."

"Take all the time you need. Call me tomorrow with questions." A rare warmth entered Jane's voice. "You should be proud. This is a big deal."

The line went dead. I stood in the hallway, phone clutched to my chest, trying to remember how to breathe.

Then I was running. Down the hall, stumbling through the door into the day room where everyone looked up at my entrance. "They bought it!" The shout was too loud, too bright for the quiet room. "The publisher—they bought my book!"

Chaos. Wyatt was there first, lifting me off my feet, spinning me until the room blurred. Then Mason was pounding my back, and Lily was squeezing my hands, and Madison was crying—hormones, she said, but she was smiling through it—and even Javi, who'd given me nothing but grief for months, pulled me into a hug that smelled like coffee and firehouse.

"What's it called?" Mason asked when the noise died down.

"Smoke and Surrender." I glanced at Wyatt, found him watching me with an expression that made my throat tight. "It's about a firefighter. And a woman who learns that sometimes the bravest thing you can do is stay."

"Think any of them are as stubborn as me?" Wyatt's voice was rough.

I smiled. "Every single one."

Wyatt

The door opened, and Cole Rivers walked in.

He looked tired—dark smudges under his eyes, uniform wrinkled like he'd slept in it. But in his hands, cradled like it was a priceless artifact, was a piece of paper covered in crayon drawings.

"From Tyler." He held it up for the room to see. "He made it at school. Wanted everyone who helped find him to have a copy."

The drawing was a masterpiece of six-year-old art. Stick figures with oversized heads surrounded by trees and what might have been mountains. In the center, a boy with brown scribbles for hair stood next to a tall figure with a red shirt—a firefighter, obviously. At the bottom, in careful letters: THANK YOU FOR SAVEING ME.

"Saving is spelled wrong," Luke said, pointing at the page.

"He's six." Cole's voice was gentle. "Cut him some slack."

The card made its way around the table, each person studying it, smiling at the earnest attempt to capture gratitude in crayon. When it reached Mason, he held it longer than the others, something softening in his expression.

"We should frame this." He looked at Cole. "Put it in the hallway with the others."

Before Cole could answer, the door opened again.

Harper Mills stood in the entrance, Tyler clutching her hand. She looked—exhausted was too kind a word. Worn. Scraped thin. Her waitress uniform was wrinkled, her hair escaping its ponytail, dark circles carved beneath her eyes.

But her chin was up. Always up.

"I wanted to come in person." Her voice was formal, careful. "To thank everyone. For what you did. For my son."

The room went quiet. Not an uncomfortable silence, but a weighted one. Everyone understood that this woman didn't want help, didn't want charity, didn't want anything that might make her feel like she owed someone.

"You don't need to thank us." Mason stood, his voice gentle. "We were just doing our jobs."

"You saved his life." Harper's grip on Tyler's hand tightened.

Tyler was scanning the room, searching for something. Someone. When his eyes landed on Cole, his whole face transformed.

"Uncle Cole!"

He broke free of his mother's grip and launched himself across the room. Cole caught him easily, lifting the boy onto his hip with the practiced ease of someone who'd done it a hundred times.

"Hey, buddy." Cole's voice changed when he talked to Tyler—softer, warmer, stripped of all professional distance. "You doing okay?"

"I drew you a picture. Did you see? That's you with the red shirt, because firefighters wear red."

"I saw. It's beautiful. Best picture I've ever gotten."

Harper hadn't moved from the doorway. Her eyes were fixed on Cole holding her son, and something complicated moved across her face. Pain. Longing. Fear.

She met Cole's gaze for half a second, then looked away.

"Tyler, we need to go." Her voice was too bright. "We have things to do."

"But I want to stay with Uncle Cole—"

"Now, Tyler."

The boy's face fell, but he kissed Cole's cheek before wriggling down. He took his mother's hand again, smaller and slower than before.

"Thank you." Harper addressed the room, not looking at anyone in particular. "All of you."

Then she was gone. Tyler waved over his shoulder until the door closed between them.

Emma

Cole stood frozen where Harper had left him, his hand still raised like he might reach after them. The look on his face—God. I knew that look. Had worn it myself for five years.

"He's got it bad." Wyatt's voice was low, meant only for me.

"She's terrified." I watched Cole finally lower his arm, watched him compose his features back into professional neutrality. But his eyes stayed on the door.

"Think he's got a shot?"

I squeezed Wyatt's hand. "If he's patient."

"Sounds familiar."

"The best things are worth fighting for." I leaned into him, let his warmth anchor me. "Someone smart told me that once."

"Yeah?" His lips brushed my temple. "Sounds like a wise guy."

"The wisest." I smiled against his shoulder. "Even if it took him five years to figure out his own advice."

Wyatt

That night, the cabin glowed.

Fire crackling in the wood stove. Lamplight pooling gold across the floorboards. Snow falling soft outside the windows, catching the light from within like the whole mountain was celebrating with us.

Emma lay beside me in the loft bed, her head on my chest, her hair spread across my skin like silk. Her breathing was slow, even, but I knew she wasn't sleeping. Neither of us could sleep. Not tonight.

"Thank you." Her voice was barely above a whisper.

"For what?"

"For helping me find my ending."

I traced patterns on her bare shoulder, following the path of her shoulders. All of her. Mine to touch and protect and worship.

"We found it together."

She lifted her head, and in the lamp's amber glow, her eyes were luminous. Green and gold and everything I'd spent five years trying to forget. Everything I'd spend the rest of my life trying to deserve.

"I love you." She said it simply, like it was the easiest thing in the world. Like she hadn't spent years building walls against exactly this feeling.

"I love you." The words didn't feel big enough. Never would.

I reached toward the nightstand, found the small box I'd hidden there three days ago. My fingers felt thick, clumsy against the velvet. Nerves. Stupid, after everything. But my heart hammered against my ribs like it wanted out. This mattered. More than any fire, any rescue. This was everything.

"Wyatt?" Emma pushed herself up on her elbow. "What—"

I opened the box.

The ring was simple. A single diamond in a vintage setting I'd found at an antique shop in Ridgeway. Nothing flashy. Nothing that would feel wrong on her practical, beautiful hands.

"I know what you'd be signing up for," I said, my voice rough. "The late nights, the worry, the risks. The rotting deck and the dripping faucet and all the broken things we'll have to fix together. This cabin, this life—none of it's perfect. But it's real. And I can't do it without you. Marry me, Emma."

Silence. One beat. Two.

Then Emma was laughing—not the polite laugh she gave strangers, but the real one. The one that scrunched up her nose and made her eyes disappear and transformed her entire face into pure joy.

"Yes." She was crying too, tears sliding down her cheeks even as she smiled. "Yes, I love it. I love you. Yes to building something real.""

I slid the ring onto her finger. It fit perfectly—because of course it did. Because some things were simply meant to be.

She pulled me down to her, and the kiss tasted like tears and forever and home.

Emma

Later—much later—I lay in the dark and listened to Wyatt breathe.

The fire had burned down to embers. The snow had stopped falling. Outside the window, stars blazed in numbers impossible to count, and the mountains stood silent witness to this moment, this life, this choice.

On my laptop, closed and sleeping on the desk below, waited the final pages of my manuscript. The title page I'd written just this morning:

SMOKE AND SURRENDER

A Novel by Emma Reed

And beneath that, the dedication I'd agonized over for hours before the words finally came:

For the smoke jumper who taught me that the bravest thing you can do is stay.

And that real love isn't found in perfect moments, but built in imperfect ones.

Tomorrow, I'd send it to Jane. Tomorrow, I'd start planning a wedding and figuring out how to fix a leaky faucet and learning what it meant to build a life instead of just survive one.

But tonight—tonight I let myself simply be.

Emma Reed. Writer. Fiancée. Home at last.

Through the window, the cabin glowed against the darkness—warm light spilling from within, smoke rising straight from the chimney, two lives intertwined beneath its roof. Home. Family. Forever. The words weren't just a dream anymore.

Not perfect. Not a fairy tale. Just real. Just ours. Just beginning.

Embers To Inferno

♥

Get the first book in the series, the story of James and Madison Drake for free!

Go To: books.vabrowning.com/wildfire-hearts-prequel

About the author

♥

V.A. Browning writes contemporary romance that sizzles with workplace tension and authentic emotional depth. Her passion for storytelling was born from years of being a voracious reader who devoured romance novels by the stack, always searching for stories that balanced smart, capable characters with the messy, wonderful reality of falling in love. After spending over a decade in the hospitality industry, she discovered that the high-pressure, fast-paced world of hotels and restaurants provided the perfect backdrop for the kind of intense, slow-burn romance she loves to read—and write.

Her novels draw directly from her professional experience, bringing insider knowledge to stories about driven characters who find love in the most unexpected places. V.A. specializes in workplace romance featuring competent, passionate people who are masters of their professional domains but complete disasters when it comes to matters of the heart. She believes the best love stories happen when two people let their carefully constructed armor crack just enough to let someone else in, and she's particularly drawn to exploring how cultural heritage and family legacy shape the way we love.

When she's not crafting the perfect enemies-to-lovers dynamic or perfecting a hero's swoon-worthy declaration scene, V.A. can be found in her cozy home office overlooking her garden, usually with a diet coke within arm's reach and her two rescue dogs—a mischievous Whippet named Louie and a silly Boxer named Rocky—sprawled at her feet. Her ideal Sunday involves farmers market visits for fresh flowers and artisanal coffee, followed by afternoon sewing sessions where she creates quilts from vintage fabrics she's collected over the years. She's a firm believer that the best stories, like the best meals, are meant to be savored slowly.

V.A. is passionate about representing authentic cultural experiences in her work. She lives in Oklahoma with her two dogs, an ever-growing collection of fabric scraps, and enough romance novels to stock a small bookstore. She's currently working on her next novel, another workplace romance that promises to deliver the same blend of professional competence, cultural richness, and irresistible romantic tension that readers expect from her stories. When readers ask her about her writing philosophy, she always says the same thing: every reader deserves a happily-ever-after that feels both swoon-worthy and real, featuring characters who are passionate, flawed, and deeply, beautifully human.

Learn about all the books she has available at www.nickannypublishing.com/va-browning/

www.ingramcontent.com/pod-product-compliance
Lightning Source LLC
LaVergne TN
LVHW091134080826
845145LV00008B/2149
9781971109022